DEVIANT ANGEL

THE ANGEL SERIES BOOK 3

JO WILDE

REFLECTION

*L*ooking back throughout the short years of my twenty-two years of life, I, Stephanie Ray Collins, never dreamt that my journey would've ended at this very spot. Looking down the barrel of my enemies, I knew my demise was imminent. Even a genetically engineered angel couldn't have seen what was to come. I thought I had as much a chance as anyone, living a normal life, free to decide my own destination. I was dead wrong.

The Illuminati would never retract their ironclad claws from my flesh. I was their prized treasure and my sticker was far too valuable for them to ever let go of me. I may be a piece of property to the Family but *this* piece wasn't going down without an old fashion fight, but first... I had an uprising to go to.

The world had gone to hell in a handbasket. The system we once knew and depended on from the simplest task as getting the Sunday newspaper had come to a screeching halt. Every little minuscule part of our socialism, economy, and commerce had gone rogue. Famine blanketed the countryside like a frozen winter. Folks forced from their homes to the streets, banks closed and the almighty dollar suddenly crashed. People rioting and innocent ones shot in cold blood, left to bleed out onto the streets. As if in one sweep, the United Nations collapsed in less than one day.

The new authorities under the rule of National Socialism declared *The Order* to be invoked, like martial law only far more sinister. Our old government had completely fallen. It was gone. Vanished in one night, just like the walls of Rome, our system collapsed, crumbling to the ground.

New rulers had emerged or maybe they'd been ruling all along, behind the shadows, in secret? Aidan was right. The Elite were always there watching, hiding, and waiting for their time to act. The populous were blindsided.

I recalled something that Aidan once told me-if people new the dark things that lurked in the shadows, they would go insane. At the time, I didn't understand. A lot had changed since then. Now I understood exactly what he meant. I wished I could go back to that time of ignorance.

As reality played its evil hand, the rulers had spread their poison like Hitler conquering half of Europe. Although this uprising was on a much larger scale, taking the world by sweeps and bounds.

The Illuminati had the world by its feet, but not me. I refused to give them my free will. Because of my threat and rebellion, they wanted rid of me. I reckoned, since I wouldn't join their political massacre, they viewed me as their enemy. I reckoned that any opposing threat had to be dealt with effectively… but I wasn't going down alone. *I planned to take some with me.*

It was going to be one hell of a Fourth of July in my neighborhood. This time, I was coming with my guns loaded just like the gunfight at OK-Fucking-Corral or at least that was my theory.

THROES OF CATACLYSM

I stood in the throes of cataclysm and the hard realization that I'd been duped once again ripped through me. My gaze dropped down to the ring that embellished his middle finger, the diamond eye that betrayed his identity as the faceless boy... *my beguiling adversary*. A deadly mistake on his part!

With complete certainty, I knew what I must do next. It was like the walk of doom. *Mine*. I scoffed.

Fuck 'em.

Aidan froze. Sweat beaded his forehead. My pendulous knives hovered dangerously at his throat. The cold blades obeyed my command. I narrowed my eyes at Aidan. He knew only one slight slip, and my knives would finish him off. I smelled his fear, and I reveled in it.

Rage surged forth deep within my core, and it obeyed. The winds whipped through as I unleashed my essence, an inauspicious place where I did not recognize myself.

As if we stood in amidst of a tornado, my powers soared and the tempest grew fiercer. Everything began twirling at warp speed. The winds howled encircling Aidan and me as if we were its prey. Trees snapped back and forth violently.

Focusing on my enemy, I reigned back my powerful essence as it gnarled in protest. I asked in a voice unknown to my ears, a voice of a true and deadly *Zophasemin*. "I'm going to ask you this once," my voice echoed. "Don't lie to me, druid," I warned in a calm, steel voice. "It was you and Sally all along. The two of you framed me!"

Aidan's mouth opened to speak, but it seemed the cat had taken his tongue.

"After all this time, you hid in the shadows of anonymity like a yellow-back *coward* with that damn needle, full of God-knows-*what*!" I hissed through gritted teeth. "I remember your diamond ring." My eyes fixed on his third finger, the ring glimmered in the sunlight, gold diamonds marking an eye. I nodded at it. "It's quite unique. Though, it's hideous." I snarled.

As rage embraced my internal war, I began to toy with Aidan. With a flick of the wrist, another knife appeared pointing straight at his groin. I taunted him with a wicked smile.

The glint in his blues confirmed his fraught. I knew that I'd never become a victim to *him* ever again and I delighted in that little insight. Aidan didn't dare flinch, not even a twitch. He was wise not to trust me. Hell, I didn't trust myself at this point.

I eyed him cautiously as the dark seductress deep within my core sang its wondrous song. Intoxicated, I craved the essence like a bloodthirsty vampire craving to feed. But I fought the urge and harnessed its desires.

Answers hung on the tip of his tongue and I needed the truth. I called to him in that strange voice. "It was your hand that was behind my suffering. It was your evil magick that compelled every lawman and judge in the state of Louisiana to convict me. You were the mastermind behind my fate, sending me off to an asylum where they left me lying in my own piss and vomit, under a constant drug induced stupor by *your* orders. As I laid unconscious for months on end, unaware, my child grew within me." My voice broke from the gut-wrenching pain that consumed me. "After I gave birth, you *ripped* my baby from me, denying a mother of her own child. You destroyed everything *I* loved!" Electricity coursed through my body as lightning struck a tree and snapped it in two. "Tell me *this* is not true!" I screamed with spittle spewing. My madness was more than a simple emotion. I was a mother aching to cradle her child, a child I'd never had the chance to know, a mother seeking justice.

Aidan stayed silent for a moment.

"Tell me, NOW!" I demanded. I wanted to rip his heart right out of his chest and set it ablaze. Yet, I held the essence back. I was in control... *not him.*

"Yes, it's true!" he admitted, his eyes wide with alarm. "It's all true!" Aidan bellowed. "Everything is true! Sally and I are married. We married two centuries ago. The girl lied to you. She's immortal," he rambled as if he was standing before a priest.

"Stop! I don't care, druid. Tell me why you framed me?" I stared at this stranger as my stomach winced from his atrocities. How could I have ever loved this man?

"Wait! I'll tell you!" Aidan exclaimed, losing what little courage he had. "Before you run your bloody knives through me at least give me the opportunity to explain." Without thinking, he flinched, and my knives inched closer. He pressed his head tight against the tree as he pleaded. "Wait! I'll tell you everything."

Unexpectedly, I heard a deep laugh. I tilted my chin sideways, catching the Cajun standing only a few paces behind me, smirking. He nodded to Aidan. "This one deserves death. He does not respect women, *non!* This pig murdered my sister!" The Cajun growled. "He got her drunk and had his way, this one did. That murderous bastard used his black magick on her. His puppets... the Law Enforcement claimed she committed suicide. It was lies! All lies. *My sister* would've never taken her life." The Cajun belted out; loathing filled his voice. "If you like... I will happily dispose of this filthy baggage for you. Gotta gator out back that's hungry." A wicked smile touched his lips.

Then, it occurred to me. "What did your sister look like?"

"A lot like me only a higher pitched voice." Sarcasm poured from his perilous voice. "Adaline was about your height, sixteen, dark hair, and dark skin... very beautiful. She was good. Never in trouble, full of life. She had plans, that one, college, husband, and children. Adaline was full of dreams." The Cajun's eyes moistened. "The police found my sister's body in the alley across from the Catfish diner. It was the last place she'd been seen alive. The authorities are liars. I spit on 'em!" The Cajun lurked forward and placed his hand on his gun holster, fingers tight around its hilt as he continued, "Funny how things bite you in the ass. My peeps thought they were doing a good thing. They wanted Adaline away from the thugs of the city." The Cajun's face hardened. "They moved her to the small town of Tangi where that sociopath lived."

Emitting only a cold stone face, Aidan exhibited no remorse. The word *savage* came to mind.

I remembered the girl at the diner where my mother worked. She was wasted drunk hanging on Aidan. I had just had a huge argument with Sara. Aidan had caught me before I'd left on my bike. He'd arranged for Jeffery to pick the girl up and take her home. Could he have lied about that too? My incensed eyes cut back to Aidan. "Is this *true*?" I carefully eyed my captive. He lingered a moment as if he were conjuring up a lie. "I sent her home with Sam."

"Wait! I thought Jeffery had picked her up." Could he had been lying to me? Come to think about it, I didn't see Jeffery in the driver's seat. In fact, no one got out of the car.

My suddenly iced.

"The diner?" Aidan's brows pleated as if he had a sudden onset of amnesia. "I don't recall having Jeffery waste gas on a drunk girl."

I narrowed my eyes suspiciously. When did Aidan ever forget anything? "You don't remember?"

"Why would I remember such a mundane thing as some poor drunk twat's name?" His face carried no apology.

"Which one, Sam or Jeffery?" I spat out fighting against the fathom foot that pressed against my chest.

"Why the concern? She was merely a human girl." Finally, the villain revealed himself, emotions laced with arsenic.

I could hear the Cajun cursing a slew of words. "If you don't kill that bastard, I swear I will."

I craned my neck, eyes fixed on the Cajun. "Nick, back off! You'll get your turn!" I gravely promised. I whipped my eyes back at Aidan. "It looks like you have many enemies, druid."

"Get on with your barnyard trial. I have admitted to all my mishaps. You decide."

Nothing about him felt right. He exhumed the epitome of disgust. A far cry from the man I once knew and loved.

"No good deed goes unpunished, right?" I stared Aidan in the eye unlike that day he captured me. The essence rumbled deep within. I could feel the enmity begging to spew forth, and all I had to do was release its fervor on him. It'd be over just like that. Still, I couldn't do it.

Not yet.

Aidan spoke up. "You are aware as well as I am, the Family controls every living creature from the earth to the heavens, human and numinous. I've never belonged to myself. Nor do any of us, even you!" he paused. "Brave or perhaps witless, your father adventured down another path. He risked his life to leave the Family. If you ask me, he was a fool. Look what good his short-term freedom got him… buried six feet under."

"Shut up!" I stepped up, fist flexing by my side. "You don't get to speak about my father!"

"You mustn't get yourself in a tizzy, sweetheart. I am merely stating a fact." His arrogance superseded his common sense.

"Can the facts, druid! I haven't got time for your bullshit."

"Stupid, inbred! You think I'm wasting *your* time? Something you should know about *your* family… *our* family. If you defect from their sanction, you are as good as dead. The Family considers this apostasy, which is unforgivable. As you know, I make no excuse for my actions. I did what I had to do to survive. You can believe me or not, but I had no knowledge of where you were hanging your hat, so to speak. However, my uncle and the Family felt it was best I didn't have any contact. They claimed that a large sum of money had been exchanged for the baby. Shortly after, you disappeared with no forwarding address."

I spat at his elaborate tale. "You're *lying*! Money doesn't mean anything to me. You knew I would've never agreed to such bile."

"It's funny how fast a person can change their minds when he or she has no family and no means of support."

"You have yet to tell me why I took the fall for crimes I didn't commit."

"What does it matter now?" he shrugged. "You're free, aren't you?"

"Tell *me*!" I hissed.

Aidan exhaled a restless sigh. "Very well, if

you insist," he said in a grudging voice. "The trumped-up charges were for show. It was only a front to the public's eye. We had to make it look legit. The Family wanted the heat off their trail. There were too many lives lost to sweep it under the rug. Therefore, they decided it was in the best interest for everyone if you took the fall."

"Fall? Your family murdered people and destroyed my life. It wasn't a fall. It was an atrocity. I lost my child!"

"Doesn't the end justify the means?"

There I had it, the worm in the apple. "No! Aidan, it doesn't," I bellowed.

"Look! Sorry to offend, but that's how my world operates. A few lives lost for the greater good."

I almost charged him, but somehow, I held my feet planted to the ground. "What about our daughter?" My voice broke, "Dawn?"

"What about her?"

"Did our child's death justify your *fucking* means?"

Aidan held his tongue for a brief moment, and then he answered. "I supposed she became collateral damage." A thirst for blood surged through me. I wanted him dead! To keep from unhinging my fury, I drove one knife through his right shoulder.

Aidan screamed out from the sharp stab. "You fucking bitch! If I get loose from here. I'm going to kill you myself!"

Silently communicating, I ordered my blades to still until further orders. They obeyed, hovering in Aidan's face.

Aidan was my captive now. He was pinned against the tree as blood trickled down his arms and chest. His once crisp, white shirt changed into a deep crimson and with each breath he took, his face deepened in agony.

Good! His heart may be a cold stone but at least, he was feeling pain. I flashed a satisfying grin. "I hope you bleed like the swine that you are."

"I had no way of knowing if you were in Tim-buck-fucking-two or at the Bahamas living it up with some fruity drink on the beach."

"You lie."

"You're right!" he threw at me like shooting bullets. "I should've looked further into your whereabouts, but I had to protect Dawn. I was backed into a corner, sweetheart. It's the truth. I swear!"

"If you cared for our child so much, then why did you let your family take Dawn's life?"

I swallowed the lump that choked my pain. I wasn't going to cry, I wasn't going to cry. I repeated inwardly to myself.

"My uncle and the others in charge informed me that Sally and I would be raising the child. We'd teach her magick and our traditions. The family's long term goal had never changed. They wanted immortality.

I repeated my question. "If what you say is true, then why did they take Dawn's life?" I gritted through my teeth.

"It was not until I tried to escape with Dawn did the family turn on me. Sally ratted me out to the Family. I knew better than to trust that bitch." Aidan sneered.

"Yet, you trusted Sally enough to join her diabolical scheme to take me down."

"That's where you are wrong! I didn't get a say."

"Why are you still alive?"

Aidan's lips pressed tight and then he relented. "I remain useful to them."

"Like how?"

"The Family knows I can find you."

"They know your whereabouts?"

"My uncle bugged my jeep. Don't worry, Van or the Family won't come for you unless I defect or you murder me." His voice seemed stiff as if he'd been rehearsing lines for a Broadway play.

Holy geez! I'd put everyone into danger. I stared at him puzzled. "The Aidan I once knew would've never allowed this to happen."

"Don't blame me. Your lover boy has left a vapor trace that the Family can see miles away."

"You're lying!" I stepped closer. "Val would never be so careless. But *you*... coming here with a tracking device attached to your damn jeep takes the cake!" I wheeled on my heels, my gaze slamming into the Cajun. I shouted, as my voice spewed with panic. "Get under his jeep and find that damn tracker. Destroy it!" Then I shouted over at Jeffery and Dom. They'd gathered outside on the porch watching in silence. "Get your things. We gotta get moving *fast*. The Family will be sending their forces." I turned back to Aidan, our eyes locked. I had one more lie to uncover. "If you can track me, then why didn't you find me at Haven Hospital?"

"You may find this hard to believe, but it's the truth. The Family cast a spell. A recherché spell that blocks my sensory." His lies rolled off his tongue like sweet nectar. "It was not until you came to stay with Dom and Jeffery that I was able to find you. The Family used you as a decoy to pull me out of hiding. I underestimated them." Aidan jerked from the festering knife stuck in his shoulder. The old blood had dried his shirt as the fresh blood spread farther down his chest.

"Why should I believe you?"

"Because it's the truth!" He spewed, desperation marked his tone. "I want you back. Why is that so hard to believe?"

I scoffed. "And what? Sally, you and I all live happily ever after under the same roof?"

"I don't love Sally. I never have. I'd ditch her in a heartbeat to be with you. Besides, she's untrustworthy."

My brow shot up. "I could say the same about you."

"Like I said, I do have flaws." His voice seemed weaker. The pain was getting worse.

The soft Stevie wanted to run to him and throw her arms around his neck, but the hard Stevie preferred a daggered rammed through his lying, black heart. "Stop it! Stop saying those things to me. You do not get to whisper sweet nothings in my ear after you and your damn family destroyed my life. Everything that has ever meant anything to me, you have taken. The only thing I have in my heart for you is contempt." Calm rage poured from my voice.

Then I recalled a druid spell. One I inherited from Aidan when we had infused ourselves together. I began to chant, arms spread like an eagle's wings, calling to the elements, and demanding their powers.

"Est a tangle textu nos weave, oh quam nos decipio, nostrum pectus pectoris repletus per lugeo, nos must aufero is sceleris, a rutilus lux lucis mitis weaved, permissum suus subluceo take temerarious inter redimio him ut is nemus oh sic angustus si is wiggles retineo him anhelo!"

As my voice rose above the rising tempest, black, menacing clouds gathered. Thunder roared, and lightning streaked the sky. In the blink of an eye, a glowing rope materialized, snaking around Aidan's body, binding him to the tree. His eyes flew wide open. "Don't kill me!" he shrieked.

"You're not getting off that easily." I flashed him a dark grin. I thought at this point that I'd stepped off into the world of never, a land that had never been touched. I had to admit, there was something exalting about this all-knowing power. It made me feel alive, electrifying.

I spotted Jeffery and Dom embraced in each other's arms with the look of fear. Even the Cajun stood back eyeing me cautiously.

"What's wrong?" My eyes cut to Dom and Jeffery and then to the Cajun.

Jeffery spoke up in a worrisome tone. "Boo, go look at your face." His gaze quickly pulled away. "My face?" Alarm trickled over me. My hand shot straight to my cheek. Something was wrong. The strange texture of my skin was thick, like molten rock. The surface was hard and rough. I darted to the closest mirror ... Aidan's jeep.

When I peered into the small mirror, hysteria seized my mind. I froze, astounded. Staring back at me was a hideous creature glaring at me in mock horror. Instantly, my hands flew to my face as bloodcurdling screams escaped my lips. "What have I've done?" I whaled.

My face had warped into a sick green with mounting wrinkles. My teeth had turned black as ink. My eyes were yellow. The creature in the mirror was as frightening as it was hideous. I collapsed to the ground, rocking back and forth sobbing. "I'll never use my powers again!

I'll never wish evil upon anyone ever!" I ranted, through streaming tears. I didn't want anyone to see me like this. I tried covering my face with my hands.

Without warning, I felt a gentle hand on my shoulder. The Cajun had come to my side. Without a word uttered, he gathered me gently into his arms and carried me inside. He ventured down a narrow hall and into a dim bedroom, and gently laid me down on a bed, covered with a red patched quilt. I was in the same room before, dim lighting, a small dresser and a nightstand with a lamp setting on it.

As soon as the Cajun set me free, I shied away, with my back to him. The monstrosity that had consumed me repulsed my entire being. I couldn't stand for anyone to see me like this. I laid there heaving with painful tears while every regret I'd ever felt plowed its way through my mind. I wept not just for the ugliness that I'd become, but also for the loss of my child and for the abomination that resided within me.

All the rage.

I felt I was dying inside.

Then, out of the haze of my nightmare, a voice brought me back. "Look at me!" The

Cajun spoke in a tender voice. "Come on *belle fille!*"

While dread twisted my gut, I eased up into a sitting position. I kept my face down and hidden with my hands and hair.

The Cajun's gaze felt like tiny needles stabbing me simultaneously. I despised him for seeing me like this, ugly and an abomination. "Don't call me that! I'm hideous!" Among other emotions, a deep sense of shame robbed me of any dignity.

"Don't hide your face." He tugged at my hands.

"Stop!" I jerked away. "Don't look at me!" I balled up into a fetal position with my back to the Cajun.

No matter how hard I resisted, he was relentless. "Your face has returned to normal. Look for yourself, you are still very beautiful." There was gentleness in his thick voice.

I flipped on my side facing the Cajun. My hand reached for my face. A burst of hope shot through me as I slid off the bed and darted down the hall to the bathroom. My heart pounded against my ears as I flipped the light on and went straight for the mirror.

Slowly, I reached up and lightly touched my cheeks while I stared blankly at the mock image. The girl with the green eyes, though frightened, stared back at me. Nick was right. My face had returned to normal.

I glanced up from the mirror and saw the Cajun leaning in the doorframe. A sudden rush of joy came over me as I rushed into his arms. He held me close to his chest, stroking my hair whispering soothing words in his native tongue. He held me tight for a good while, until I loosened my grip and the tears had dried. The warmth of his smile echoed in his voice. "Now you are better, *yes?*"

"Yes. Much!" I spoke shyly, dropping my gaze and pulling away from the comfort of his arms. His kindness reminded me too much of the old Aidan. The Aidan I once loved. I couldn't get involved with another man. Three wasn't a charm in my book. There would be no love interest here, not today or ever.

Giving him nothing more than a forced smile, I quickly skirted away, heading outside. I left the Cajun standing alone. He didn't like me, and I was comfortable with our toilsome friendship. It kept things simple. Right now, with everything toppling on my shoulders, simple was all I had to give.

GATOR DIVING

*J*effery and Dom had scurried about packing their personal belongings. I didn't have many possessions. I finished in less than ten minutes, throwing a few items in an army green backpack.

When I stepped outside, I noticed the tracking device laying on top of the jeep's hood. I went straight to the car and gathered the tracker in my palm, carefully examining it. The device was the size of a dime with a tiny, blinking red light. I assumed the light was the homing mechanism.

I began thinking that if we sent this thing in the opposite direction, it might buy us some time. I glanced over at Aidan. A spike of hope stirred. Luck might be on our side after all.

His eyes were fixed on me as he stood there, tied to the tree. If he so much as sneezed, the magick rope would tighten its grip like a python squeezing its prey. And for added protection, the knife in his shoulder kept him still. He wasn't wiggling out of that bind any time soon.

I reckoned that was the perks of being a genetically engineered angel. Though, I had no idea how I'd conjured up the rope. It was as amazing as it was frightening. I still preferred a bat. Much simpler and just as effective.

As much as I hated the notion, Aidan would have to remain as my prisoner. If his internal radars pinpointed my location, we all were sitting ducks.

I especially worried for the safety of Dom and Jeffery. If the guys landed in Van's hands, I didn't want to begin to think what he'd do. It seemed nothing had changed. Van was still hell bent on finishing me off. He'd stoop to any measure to draw me out.

That meant he'd use the guys for leverage. If Jeffery and Dom ended up hurt or worse, I wouldn't be able to live with myself. I had to get them out of the line of fire and to a safe place. The problem was, where?

Right now, anyone associated with me was in imminent danger. Even more of a reason why I needed to find a safe place for the guys. I'd figure it all out, but for now, we needed to get moving and find a new hideout and the sooner, the better.

In the break of silence, a twig snapped. In a deadly flash, I drew my knife. It hovered over my head ready to charge. When my eyes landed on the person approaching, I relaxed, sending my magical knife back to its sheath. I exhaled a tight breath. It was only the Cajun.

"Donnez-moi le dispositif!" (Give me the device!) He demanded.

"What are you going to do?" I asked, unsure if I should trust him.

"Ole Saint Nick has some tricks up his sleeve." His dark eyes glistened with mischief.

I snorted a short laugh. Someone really needed to talk to him about referring to himself in third person. "Oh *really*," I said. "This I gotta see."

The Cajun snatched the tracker out of my palm and off he went in three long strides to my one. Sprinting to keep up, I followed closely behind him, heading straight for the river at the backside of the house. A sense of dread came over me. I hoped he knew what he was doing. I might be able to throw a little magick here and there, but that swamp, bayou or hell water, scared the crap out of me.

In one swift motion, the Cajun pulled a knife from his hip, sliding it between his lips and tugging off his jeans, down to the bare. Without missing a beat, he dove into the murky water as if an Olympian swimmer had gone Tarzan. His masterstrokes were precise and fluid.

Jeffery and Dom had gathered beside me, watching in silence at the Cajun's head bobbing up and down, as he glided with ease across the steady stream.

Jeffery wedged his skinny ass between Dom and me to the front. "What the hell is that crazy hunk-of-loveliness doing in that nasty river?" Jeffery craned his neck, eyeballing the fully nude man. The three of us stood frozen, eyes glued to the Cajun. The starkness in our faces revealed our alarm.

I always had a healthy fear of the bayou. I respected its savageness. It was a haven to creatures of the dark. As for the rest of us, if we were smart, we keep our distance.

I had to admit, there was a part of me that

felt enamored over the Cajun's dare-deviltry. Though, however brave he might appear, it was a reckless stunt that could get him killed.

I stood holding my breath, eyes glued to his glistening muscles flexing in the water. I watched in awe and horror as the water commenced splashing violently like an eruption from beneath.

All at once, a huge scaly tail emerged, following a white belly, churning in the roily water, thrashing this way and that. We caught a glimpse of the Cajun rolling under the water in a tug of war with the gator. His knife glinted from the sunlight as he clenched it between his teeth. I stifled a gasp, daring not to make a sound. Jeffery was doing enough screeching for all of us.

The gator fought furiously. Yet the Cajun clung to the back of the beast, riding it like a bronco in a rodeo. With each death-dealing spin, he held the creature's snout tightly shut as he and the long-tail reptile pirouetted in a fierce battle.

"Uh-huh, it's not every day you see a naked man battlin' an alligator." Jeffery stretched his neck over Dom's shoulder to catch a look at the Cajun's glimmering backside popping from the water.

"Jeffery, shut up!" I nudged him with my elbow.

Dom flashed him a warning, but remained quiet.

"Oookay!" he threw his hands to his hips. "I'm just sayin'." Jeffery pursed his lips, giving me the evil eye. I snorted a laugh and turned my attention back to the commotion in the water.

We watched helplessly from the bank as the Cajun continued wrestling the mighty creature. With no warning, a dead silence swathed the forest. Even the birds stopped chirping. Not even the soft hum of a Cicada among the trees. The river calmed, and a soft trickle meandered downstream.

All at once, movement stirred. Two perfectly round eyeballs peeked the surface of the murky water. It was the gator drifting aimlessly down the river stream as if he'd had a lazy day sunbathing.

We all three gasped in fear as alarm hit me like a head on collision with a freight train. The Cajun hadn't surfaced. In a fit of fury, I tossed my boots off and started stripping off every stitch of clothing down to my underwear.

The white of Jeffery's eyes nearly went to

the back of his head, "What the hell are you doing?" he shrieked, grabbing my arm.

"I don't want my clothing to hold me down. I have to save Nick!"

"Stevie, the alligator!"

"Dom, I've gotta go after him!" The Cajun was an idiot, but he doesn't deserve to die. Yet, I wasn't letting his rash decision slip past me, either. I couldn't promise that he'd remain intact when I got my hands on him.

Just as I started to plunge headfirst into the foul water, the Cajun's head popped up with his knife still gripped between his teeth, swimming toward us.

A rush of relief came over me. I was happy to see him and the thought of jumping in the river didn't seem like an unthinkable task.

When the Cajun pulled himself onto the bank, my mood quickly shifted to a boiling stew. "What the hell were you thinking? You could've gotten yourself killed!" I shoved his chest hard. "We don't have time for such recklessness!"

"Ah, how sweet!" Water dripped down his face as he flashed his white pearly smile. "I had no idea you cared so much, Red."

My face blazed as I fired back. "You arrogant son of a " The Cajun interrupted.

"Non!" he wagged his finger, tsking me. "You leave *mon mère* (my mother) out of this." he snarled. "I solved the *problème*. The device is deep in the belly of the alligator. It should keep those *bâtard* busy for hours. Perhaps days."

"You-you wrestled that six-foot-something beast."

"Oui! Just call me the gator whisperer." He slapped me on my back as if I were one of the boys. "See... Saint Nick is smart. Yes?" The Cajun tapped his temple with his finger.

We all stood there gaping at him. I thought I was impulsive. The Cajun had me beat.

"We need to leave *now!* Got any ideas?"

"Oui, we can go to my place. Tie your boyfriend up in the jeep and you ride with me." As his eyes slowly roamed over my body, my face blistered. I'd forgotten about stripping down to my bra and panties. In a huff, I snatched up my clothes and stalked off with a slew of curse words trailing behind me.

LIES UNVEILED

Sitting on the back of his damn bike and clinching my arms around his waist had not been my idea. In fact, I despised it. The Cajun reeked of swamp water. It had been bad enough for me to cling to his half-naked body. Granted, with the dirty water slapping my face, I was at the end of my patience. I preferred eating bugs over coughing and gagging on the stale water that tasted like rotten fish.

Watching the Cajun snorkel at my uncomfortable plight only escalated my pissy mood. The man detested me. His bold grin across his face proved my suspicions.

Dom drove the Jeep and Jeffery sat in the passenger seat, doing his usual directing. I had battened down Aidan in the back with the magickal rope. He was nicely snug, and knew better than to attempt breaking free. My knives hovered evenly with Aidan's neck.

Despite everything, my heart tugged at my decision. I tossed a glimpsed over my shoulder at my prisoner. I no longer knew this man. Where did that Aidan go? The man who risked his own life for mine.

That Aidan was gone, and in his place, a soulless monster resided. I mustn't forget that the present Aidan had proven where his loyalties lie. The Illuminist had their poisonous claws in him. I realized that Aidan inherited his family's traits.

Setting aside my guilt, I had to keep my family safe. Perhaps giving myself up would get the Family off everyone else's tail? The guys would be fine with the Cajun. They were no threat to the Family, but staying with me, I feared would put a target on their backs.

I desperately wished Val were here. He'd know what to do. I was more helpless than a toddler. Just because I had the ability of a powerful angel didn't mean anything. The few tricks I had up my sleeve weren't enough. I didn't have the supernatural smarts to get us through this. I was no match for the Family. None of us were.

Strange now that I thought about it. I'd give away every bit of my magickal birth to be an ordinary girl again. Looking back, struggling for food and a roof over my head and even having my crazy mom by my side, sounded like a little piece of heaven compared to now.

I wished I could go back to blissful ignorance, thinking I was human, benighted to the harsh world's reality.

In my world, fairytales weren't for the faint hearted. It was far too sinister and far too deadly. I shuddered. Gosh, how I wanted my dad right now. Nevertheless, I knew that wasn't going to happen, and yearning for the impossible meant disappointment and a huge distraction. It was time that I put my big-girl panties on and got with the program. Impulsive Stevie had to die, and strategic, warrior Stevie had to step up to the plate and take charge.

I turned back facing the Cajun's head. Thankfully, from the wind drying him off, he wasn't slinging mud in my face any longer.

My mind began to trail back to Nick's grandmother, Mable. She hit the nail on the head and was right about Val. He never was my true boyfriend. I thought he was the one. Then he left me here, earthbound, and defenseless.

Val really thought the Cajun could protect me. I didn't see how. Yet what other choice did I have right now? I had to give him credit. Regardless of how much he despised me, he'd stuck to his word helping us. No wonder Val depended on him.

Loneliness swallowed my sigh. I was alone with no back up from any one of my kind. Even after Val and I had broken up, I somehow felt he'd find his way back to me. We'd work through the issues of the Zophasemin's prejudice. I now knew how wrong I was. Chances of that happening were zero. Val had left this realm, abandoning his human body and returning to his natural form, a spiritual creature.

Strange how I was the same race as Val and his mighty warriors. Though, I couldn't materialize into a spirit form like the rest of the Zophasemin nation. Unlike my fellow brothers, Val explained that I was earthbound. I'd already felt like an outsider looking through a plate glass. His words confirmed my beliefs. But where did I go? Whom could I turn to for help? I didn't belong to the human race no more than I belonged to the Zophasemin.

Artificial was the term Val used. I supposed the Zop leader viewed me as unnatural and impure as his own kind did. How could a nation accept diversity when their own leader could not? If Val had stood up for me, perhaps his race would've accepted me.

How ironic. I bled just like any extant creature, human or not. I was as real and genuine as the best. I resented the term, synthetic.

I finally came to a hard realization that Val's absence was for the best. If I hadn't pushed myself through his men to take one last look at him before he left, he would've vanished without so much as a goodbye. He knew he wasn't coming back and that I'd never see him again. Whatever we had was final. I wasn't his first priority and never was. If I was going to keep my family safe and survive this uprising, I had to keep my head on straight. Forget these men. They had brought nothing but misery to me and if I didn't get a grip, they would be the death of me and possibly the death of Dom and Jeffery. That, I couldn't fathom.

~

It seemed every road we'd traveled was paved with dirt. Deep craters marked the way with erosion by previous high waters. Good Ole Saint Nick hit every pothole in sight too. Thank God for my death grip around the Cajun's waist. He seemed not to mind. An interesting observation, I thought. I wondered how he was breathing with my hands tightly latched around his lungs. He didn't complain, and I didn't plan on letting go either. I wasn't going to die today. I'd save my death for a better cause.

I tossed another glance over my shoulder. Dom was tailgating us. The area here seemed to host some sketchy characters. I reckoned that Dom didn't want to get lost in this neck of woods and especially with Aidan.

The closeness the boys once had with their employer had dissipated. It was understandable considering the change in Aidan's behavior. The only one who could stand to be around him was Sally. I hope she didn't come looking for him. The last thing I needed was another captive.

I planned to kiss the ground once we reached our destination. This ride was torture and with *rápida Diablo* (speedy devil) flying down the byway, hitting every freaking hole, I expected my butt to be bruised tomorrow. To top it off, my lungs would be hacking up dirt for the next month. I hated the woods and the rough outdoors. I hated the swamp, the bugs, snakes, and gators. I wasn't too fond of the Cajun grinning every time he flew over a bump either.

After what seemed like an eternity, we finally pulled up to a clearing surrounded by Cypress trees down in the basin. I could see that the land was not prime soil and living down here had its hardships.

A small house stood nestled in the middle of the clearing. The cabin was built from pine with white stucco pressed between each log and stood high on pier and beam. Steep steps led up to the large wrap around porch. There was no grass, only dirt in the yard. I reckoned there was no point in planting greenery when the floods killed everything in its path.

I noticed at the side of the house a boat flipped over, tied to a post with an anchor dropped to the ground. My guess, it was to keep the boat in one place when the floods rushed through. Farther down, toward the back of the house, a ramp led up to the house, I assumed it was for his bike.

It was apparent the work of love that went

into building the home. The cabin was solid, most likely sturdy enough to withstand the frequent storms in this God forsaken country.

When we came to a halt, I climbed off the bike and made a beeline for the sanctuary of the front porch. I climbed the steps and went straight to the rockers. I flopped down in one, and immediately a sigh of relief escaped my lips as comfort enshrouded my badly beaten backside. I smiled as my hands rubbed against the smooth arms of the chair. The wood felt cool, and the chair rocked with perfect precision, an ingenious design. I leaned back, taking in the wonderful solace of the chair and smiled to myself.

Suddenly, I heard footfalls approaching. Startled, I whipped my eyes open and my gaze landed on the Cajun. He was as bad as a little puppy, following me wherever I went. I exhaled. He was very easy on the eyes, just a little rough around the edges, which worked for him. Too bad, he didn't have a personality. I scoffed as I watched him climb the stairs, one stomp at a time.

"Must your face sour whenever you look at me? Most ladies enjoy my company," Nick bragged tossing his crooked smile at me.

"Those women are paid by the hour," I mused. I couldn't resist the jab.

"If you keep that nasty attitude no one will ever care about you," he sneered.

"Don't worry, I'm as cuddly as a porcupine!" I smiled back. Deep down, I feared he might be right.

"You are one bitter woman. I suppose if you got with him," The Cajun nodded at Aidan. "I'd be bitter too. The problem with you, is you have never had a real man. One who is willing to stick up for you and stay by your side when times get rocky. Your choice of men is no good."

"Val would be here if he could!" The Cajun had a point, but my pride got the best of me. I didn't want to admit he was right.

"*Moi*! However, he was not a man. He was a celestial being, an angel. Even if he wanted to stay, it would have never worked between the two of you. His kind does not permit such ...."

I halted that damn coonass right then and there. "Stop it! What do you know about me? You've known me for about one hot minute. Until you do, don't be so quick to judge me." By then, I was on my feet and in his face. Or somewhat. He was an astounding six foot five and I barely reached five-five.

"*Pas de problème*! (No problem) I was only trying to be nice." The Cajun threw up his palms in surrender. "I really do not care about your lovers. You probably lie still like a stump." His scornful eyes locked with mine.

"Let's get something straight, Saint Nick. As soon as I can find us a place to go, your sorry ass is relieved of duty," I hissed in his face.

"Red, I'm going to give you the same advice you have been so kind to have given *moi. Take a bath.* You stink. There's a towel and soap in the shower. It's on the back porch. Enjoy!" He smiled, but it didn't touch his deep brown eyes. I stared at him for a moment as faint laughter drifted from Aidan who remained tied to the Jeep. With a deep throaty growl, I twirled in my shoes and headed for the back porch. Nothing like a cold shower to wash off the dirt and angry steam. I had a strong hunch that this wasn't going to end well. Between the Cajun and Aidan, my nerves were grating fast. *What was Val thinking?*

I sent Jeffery off to find my bag of clothes. Luckily, he found them in the nick of time, as I'd finished showering. "Thanks, Jeff!" I reached up over the wooden enclosure, snatching up my backpack and smiled.

"Hurry up! I want to shower too. I hope you didn't take all the hot water," Jeffery mumbled, stomping off and disappearing around the corner of the porch. I shook my head, laughing.

Though there wasn't a hot and cold valve, the clean water was amazing. The shower was enclosed with crafted wood, attached to the side of the house with plumbing connected to the outdoor pipe and a wide showerhead hanging above. It was like a regular indoor shower only it was on his back porch. "Rats!" I fumbled through my bag. Just my luck, no bra. Great! No bra around a bunch of men and only a thin tee shirt to wear. Crap! No Wal-Mart to remedy that problem either. I had my dirty bra that reeked of swamp and sweat. Geez, I missed the comforts of the modern world's conveniences. Nothing I could do about it right now. I did what any woman would do, I sucked it up and decided to keep my arms folded.

In a rush, I slipped on my cut off shorts and doubled up on the thin tank tops. I figured if I wore two tops, no one would notice. I ran a hand through my hair and felt the matted tangles. My hair was a mess. I didn't care. It was the least of my worries. I grabbed my cowboy boots and slipped them on. My old western boots couldn't have been a better fit. They pretty much reached my knees. Out here in the bayou, I doubted the old leather would protect me from a gator, but it might stave off a snakebite.

Once I stepped into the house, I caught sight of a cozy fire radiating the fireplace. The sound of the kindling crackling brought back memories of a time I didn't care to revisit. I quickly started to exit the house but stalled. I'd unknowingly walked upon a conversation that appeared heated. I eavesdropped listening to the Cajun and Aidan. I knew I shouldn't be snooping. The last time I'd listened in on a private discussion, it didn't turn out well for me. Even still, I couldn't peel myself away. A deadly habit, I reckoned I had.

"You should be ashamed of yourself, rich boy." The disdain in the Cajun's tone was blistering.

"You'd be wise to mind your own business," Aidan's aversion matched the Cajun's.

"I am a good judge of character. You, ami

(friend), are rotten from the inside out. Did you take this young girl's virginity?"

Aidan answered with silence.

I heard the ire in the Cajun's words. "Of course, I should've known. You had to go and ruin this innocent girl. I have a mind to horse whip you."

"What do you know about family and duty?" Aidan snarled. "Bet you've never had to do a thing in your whole pathetic life except run your mouth and snort a keg of beer down." The narcissism in Aidan's voice was startling.

"You think you know me well," the Cajun laughed darkly.

"Don't worry about the girl. She received an ample settlement for her services."

"One thing you forget rich boy."

"And?" Aidan growled.

"All the money in the world will never bring her child back."

"She will move on." Aidan's voice resonated with a coldness that turned my blood cold. I bit my lip, reeling in my own anger.

"Are you that conceited?" the Cajun snarled. "It is your family's selfish greed that has brought mayhem to this girl. She's a fugitive because of you!"

Aidan scoffed, "Must we be gloomy?"

The Cajun spoke a calm cold voice. "I'd much

rather take a Benelli M4 semi-automatic rifle to you. Maybe before the uprising is over, I will have that opportunity."

"Get over yourself," Aidan dismissed him. "I believe my family has improved her life," Aidan contended proudly. "She can grow old and weary, never having to lift a finger ever again with her wealth."

"Setting aside the little fact that money is useless right now. You think money can erase the bad deeds you and your family have committed. You're wrong! She's only twenty-one. She has yet to live her life, and you once again have taken that from her. No wonder she is bitter. If I were her, I'd be throwing knives at every man's balls that came in close contact of me. You are a hypocrite, and you call me trash? In my book, I'd much rather be my kind of trash than yours. It is not the material things that makes men. It is the good deeds men do that makes a man. You hide behind your tainted magick." I heard feet stomping and stopping short. I peeked around the corner. The Cajun had gotten in Aidan's face. "I say come out like a man with your fist up. Let's see how long you last then, yes?" The challenge in the Cajun's voice was grave.

· · ·

I doubted Nick's blows would be as fast as Aidan's. I knew far too well how deadly Aidan could be if pushed. I had to admit, the Cajun defending my honor took me by surprise. Aidan's cavalier attitude was expected.

I needed to break this scuffle up before the Cajun got himself skinned alive. I stepped out onto the front porch. My eyes landed on the Cajun. He stood up from Aidan who was sitting in one of the rockers. My eyes drifted to Jeffery standing on the bottom steps tapping his foot nervously. Dom stood by the Jeep, pulling out his and Jeffery's bags.

All eyes fell on me. Talk about uncomfortable! The tension in the air was heavy. I blew out an awkward breath. Instead of reacting, I pretended I didn't notice and directed my attention to Nick. "Hey, what kind of vittles you got around here? I can get dinner started."

The Cajun stood up as his eyes lingered a little too long over my tank top while Aidan sat quite full of piss. Jeffery kept wiggling as though he might pee in his pants. The smartest one of all, Dom, had kept his distance from the volatile situation.

The Cajun answered, "You look good

enough to eat." He flashed his crooked smile, perfect white teeth, openly flirting with me.

"Do you mind if I go through your kitchen and see what you got to eat?" A terse smile toiled at the corner of my lips. I ignored the Cajun's compliment. He was only taunting the prisoner. I had no plans to join his little spar. I caught a glance at Aidan. Noting his angry blues, that Cajun better watch his step. An immortal druid brawling with a human, the odds were stacked against the Cajun and I wasn't too keen on the idea of having to step between those two big jugheads.

The Cajun caught my attention, disrupting my train of thoughts. "Don't worry about cooking. We're having guest coming later. Barbeque and beer. We're having a social gathering. I know some bedfellows who can help. Go rest. I'll watch the prisoner for you." The Cajun flashed a far too confident grin.

"Nick, I'm not sure that's a good idea." My lips twisted sourly.

"Damn woman! You take the joy out of a little fun for Saint Nick."

There he went speaking in third person again.

"Sorry to be a killjoy." I smiled, even though

I didn't feel it in my eyes. "Okay, a nap sounds great, but I have to do something first."

I turned to go back inside, and a few minutes later, I returned with a glass of cold water. I had no idea the last time Aidan had anything to drink and I couldn't rest until I knew he'd at least had some water. I recalled how courteous he was to me when I went to stay at his castle. I felt I owed him that much.

Standing at the last rocker, I leaned down, low, in order for our conversation to be more private. "I thought you might be thirsty." I held the drink to his lips. He sipped slowly. I hoped we could have an amiable discussion, "Aidan," I started. "I hate holding you hostage. But you leave me no other choice. I can't trust you." If I appealed to his selfishness, he might ease up. I furthered with my discussion, "If we could free our bond, I'd let you go unharmed."

I held the glass to his lips again, but he pushed his lips away and glared up at me through murderous eyes. "Sweetheart, I'm really getting tired of repeating myself." His Adam's apple bobbed. "I'm afraid you're stuck with me."

"Why do we have to continue this union when we both want separation?"

"Sorry, toots! Death is the only option we have to break the bond."

Did I hear him correctly? I fell into the rocker beside Aidan. My body went numb. "We're bound to each other forever?" I looked at him with shock, remembering his spurn.

"I suppose our bond takes a whole new meaning to ball-and-chain." His implacable expression was unnerving.

"Stop with the jokes. There has to be some way to break the curse."

"Not unless you wish to die." A satanic smile pressed against his lips. "You might as well give it up. Embrace our dark bond and accept your destiny."

"Destiny?" my brows shot up. "What destiny are you referring to?" his cocky attitude was starting to grate on me.

"Did I not explain to you or are you just too stupid to catch on?"

Aidan was pushing my buttons. His taunting was futile. I wasn't going to take his bait. "Gee, after all that angel dust you so kindly bestowed upon me, I can't say for sure. But why don't you humor me and tell me anyway. I'll be sure and take notes this time."

Aidan laughed. Disappointingly, I found his

laugh flat, not the usual infectious laugh that I once adored.

"I can't do or undo the impossible. But I'm a fair man." An expression of satisfaction showed in his eyes. "Leave with me now and all will be forgotten. Your friends will be pardoned of their treason. Save your friends and save yourself. We both know you belong with the Family, *our* family. Live like the princess you are by my side, ruling the world."

I stared into Aidan's bloodshot eyes. The sparkle had vanished. Even his skin appeared gray and pallid. "Look, I'm not leaving with you." I shook my head. "I don't want any part of the Family." I looked off into the stand of trees. "Do you want anything to eat? You're looking ill."

"Of course, I look like shit! This rope is siphoning the life out of me." Suddenly an attack of coughing came over him, wheezing, straining for breath as his face blistered. He finally managed to gain his composure enough to choke out. "I need a cigarette."

Shock stole my breath. "Since when do you smoke?"

"Never mind about what I do," he choked out. "Since you plan on keeping me tied up, go ask the basin trash for a smoke."

"You can ask him yourself. I'll get you some food."

"Fuck food. I want a cigarette!" he practically screeched.

"Whatever!" I jumped to my feet. "Starve for all I care, but I won't get you a cigarette." I turned to leave but stopped.

"Why do you torment yourself? You have the power to stop all this running and hiding."

I slowly turned to face him. "What do you mean?"

"Surrender and your friends will go unscathed. They can go free," he flashed a weak smile. "I miss us. I still love you?"

I stared at him for a moment. Repulsion churned my stomach, taking everything I had not to vomit, "I refuse to do that to Sally."

"She's simply a distraction," Aidan refuted. His smooth talk paled in comparison to the hold he once held on my heart.

"Sally thinks the two of you are a couple. You are sleeping with her."

"A man does have needs."

"Does Sally know that she's scratching your need?" I glowered at his opened decadence.

"Don't be such a rigid bitch! You once liked my affections lying in bed all day between the sheets?"

"Your memory must really be slipping from your old age. That's not how I remember it."

"Oh yes, we mostly fought."

"You can sleep with the Dalai Lama for all I care. I want my life back. Just break the curse."

"You think our bond is a curse?"

"Look! Curse or not, does it matter? You and I have changed. Or maybe I'm the one who has." Cutting ties was the only thing that made sense. "We've grown apart," I pointed out. By the disdain tainting his face, I knew he loathed my rejection even though he no more desired me than I did him.

"You forget too easily," he accused.

"I only wish that were true."

"Don't you remember our conversation about our infusion at your house?" His smile became voracious, "The spell keeps other men away. It works much like a bug repellent."

"I repel men?" I thought he was just trying to hurt me. I didn't realize he meant it literally.

Aidan smirked. "Why do you think Val never went through with sealing the deal?"

"Come again?" All at once, it was like the bell of clarity sounding off in my head. All the times that Val held back, I blamed him for not taking it to the next level.

"That's even more reason I want this curse

broken," I snapped. "You better figure out a way to break this curse or else I swear, I'll take your life myself." In the heat of the moment, I threw the rest of the iced water in his face. "Get your own damn water!" I twirled on my heels and stalked off into the house. I glimpsed up, and there stood Nick leaning against the door jam. I expected him to be laughing. To my surprise, sadness glimmered behind his eyes. As we stood briefly holding each other's gaze, neither one of us uttered a word.

At this point, I didn't have the strength to rehash this thing between Aidan and me. It was too complicated and disturbing. Rather, I brushed past him and went straight to the room with the biggest bed. Guessing from the Cajun's size, I assumed that would be his room.

After a couple of hours of sleep, my eyes popped open. My head swirled with murk, and my body ached like an old woman with rheumatoid arthritis. I blamed it on my angel magick. It had taken a toll on me. My strength felt depleted.

When my eyes drifted down to my feet, I gasped. The last time a person sat on the edge of my bed, it turned out to be a ghost, Ms. Noel. Then my eyes landed on the tear streaked face and I eased a breath.

Jeffery sat with his shoulders slumped, sobbing. I right away sat up with alarm. "Jeff, what's wrong?"

"Oh, I don't mean to wake you," he sniffled.

"No. You're fine. What's wrong?"

"What isn't wrong? We've lost our home. We all may die. That vicious Family is coming after all of us. Dom isn't well. He has heart problems, and I'm afraid he's going to drop dead. Boo, I can't lose Dom." Jeffery's tears poured. My heart dropped, and I took Jeff into my arms and embraced his quivering body. After a minute, he pulled himself together and straightened up, wiping his tear stained face.

"I know this isn't easy. I've been racking my brain trying to think of a perfect hideout for you and Dom until this uprising is over." I chewed on my bottom lip, thinking. "I'll talk to Nick and see if he has any ideas. Right now, we have no defense. We haven't a clue to what's going on out there. We have no outside sources to update us on the current situation. Hell, we don't even have our cell phones anymore. I don't know if we can even drive through town without getting killed."

"It's the not knowing that is worrying Dom and me." Jeffery choked through tears.

"I'm terribly sorry for bringing you and Dom in the middle of this mishap. I've put you in danger."

"Stop that! Don't blame yourself." Jeffery wiped his face with the back of his hand. This ain't your fault, boo." Jeffery squeezed my hand, "Those mofos had this foolery planned eons ago. Gurrrl, don't you blame yourself for one minute. Dom and I will stand beside you no matter what. We love you like a daughter, and I knows that love is returned," then he paused, shaking his head. "It's different with Aidan. Don't get me wrong, Dom and I love Aidan. But we knows to keep our distance and our opinions to ourselves. And this new Aidan, actin' like a fool, I see now that we never knew him at all. We hate every nasty thing he's done to you. For that, we is mad as hell at him."

"Don't go wagging your finger at him. He's dangerous and unpredictable. He's not the same, Jeffery." I tightened my lips, feeling an urge of ire. "Why is that? I don't get it."

"Gurrrlfriend, Dom and I have been wonderin' the same thang," Jeffery huffed out a long breath. "It's like some stranger has stepped into Aidan's skin. I don't recognize this man."

"I know what you mean. If Sam was alive and knowing Sam's cloning abilities, I'd be asking questions. But Sam's dead. I witnessed his death with my own eyes. That theory of cloning Aidan died with Sam." I raked my fingers through my hair.

"Dom and I've been talkin'." Jeffery jumped up and shut the door and quickly returned, sitting back down on the edge of the bed with me. "If we didn't know any better, Aidan's actin' a lot like his uncle, Van."

"Van? No way!" My breath stalled.

"I knows how ugly his uncle can get. Dom knows it too."

I bit my bottom lip. "There's no way Van could be masquerading as Aidan. I overheard the old man say to the brotherhood that he's mortal and doesn't have any special abilities. Van is not Aidan's actual uncle. They're not blood relative nor does Van have druid magick."

"Dom and I figured that out real quick. Van always seemed different. You know, cut from a different cloth."

"I think you're right, but I think Van has a

hold over Aidan. Maybe that's why Aidan's acting so strange."

"Maybe? Van is sneaky as a snake. I wouldn't put anything past him."

"We're wasting time speculating. I need to find a safe place for you and Dom. The sooner the better too!"

"You is comin' with us, right? It ain't your fight either." Jeffery knew how to make a good argument.

My brows wrinkled, and my heart tugged. "Jeff… it is my fight. I'm fighting for my freedom, for *our* freedom. I don't belong to myself."

"You talk like you is their property!"

"Think about it, Jeff," I paused. "The Family created me. I don't even have a biological mother. I'm not human!" I sucked in a deep breath. I was stuck between a rock and a hard spot. No one could save me. Not even God, if there was such a person.

"Now you're actin' cray-cray! You is more human than most!"

I smiled, but only to ease my friend. "You're sweet! I might look human, but technically, I'm an experiment, a genetically engineered creature to fit whatever mold they intended for me. I have no rights. The Illuminist has ownership of me."

"What?" Jeffery shrieked.

"I haven't told anyone about this, but the Illuminist tagged Mom and me."

"What you mean tagged?" Jeffery's eyes bugged.

"It's alien technology known as implants. I can't be certain, but I think during the lab trials, the scientist inserted a tiny alien micro-magnetic device in my mom and me. The Family has been keeping tabs on us all my life. I fear the microchip is still active. If I'm right, no matter where I go the Family can find me."

"Oh lord, have mercy! *Jesus* take me home! We gotta get that thang out of you."

"You can't without killing me."

"Sweet Mother of God! We need to bring in the cavalry." Sweat dotted Jeffery's forehead as he patted his forehead with the end of the blanket.

"If the device is still working, then it's pointless for me to hide. I'm like a beacon in the middle of a shit-storm. Even if Aidan and I break our bond, his family might still be able to detect my location." Chills bristled my neck. "Aidan once told me that the tags have dissolved. I have a gut feeling he lied and if so, that means anyone hanging around me is at risk."

"Gurrrl, there's got to be another way."

"I don't see how," I shrugged. I jumped up and stood in front of the window. The worried expression in Jeffery's face was too much for me to bear.

"Damn, Val! He ought to be 'ere for you." Jeffery's anger and frustration came through loud and clear.

I looked over my shoulder at Jeffery. "No need to blame Val," I said. "It's not his fault. His priority is to the Zophasemin nation."

"Isn't that your race too?"

"It's different for me. I was man-made. The others came from divine creation. Anyway, that doesn't matter now," I shrugged. "The Zops consider me impure. That's not ever going to change."

"Impure, my sweet ass!"

"It's complicated." Revisiting the memories were so acute, it was like physical pain.

"Boo, Dom and I are not abandoning you."

"I know you want to stay with me to protect me, but let's be honest. We're not going up against just ordinary people. We might be facing a nation of supernatural demons. So, you guys staying with me would be suicide and I can't let that happen. That's non-negotiable." I'd put my foot down to that.

"Gurrrl, I ain't arguing with you. We're not leaving you!" Jeffery pursed his lips and folded his arms. He was stubborn as a jackass and cuddly as a puppy. I loved my Jeffery. "Let's change the subject!"

Jeffery's eyes lit up. Oh lord! "Okay." With Jeffery, one never knew what was going to come out of his mouth. "Don't be hatin' me for saying this, but I like Nick. He may be human and rough around those delicious edges, but I think that's what you need. If there's anything that I know best … is when a man is juicy for another. And boo, that man is thick pulp-juicy for you."

I burst into laughter, and it felt good too. A nice change. "Oh yeah, the Cajun's juicy alright. He's so juicy, he'd like to feed me to the gators."

"Now I didn't say you didn't rub him the wrong way. I don't think he's accustomed to women like you. Have you got a real good look at that man? Uh huh, he is one tall dark drink."

"Jeff!" I held my palm up. "Please!" I rolled my eyes.

"Don't be ridiculous. That man is fine! With that deep chocolate hair and his yummy brown eyes gleaming at you and have you seen the six pack he's packin'?" Jeffery nearly started drooling.

I tried stifling a laugh, but I lost the battle shamefully. "Jeffery don't be getting bugged-eyed over the candy Cajun. I don't want to whoop his ass on your behalf."

"Don't worry gurrrl. I've been a butler for more than half my life. I knows how to look without really lookin'."

"Jeffery, that's too much information!" I giggled as I swatted my friend's arm. Then the mood shifted like the wind on a stormy Sunday.

"Jeff, with the way the world is going right now, the last thing I need is a boyfriend." I exhaled a long breath. "I'm still trying to get over my feelings for Aidan." I shrugged, feeling so lost in this mad world.

"You ain't meaning that Aidan out there tied up?"

I gave a curt laugh as I joined him back on the end of the bed. "Hell, no!" I paused. "No, it's the old Aidan I miss. There's a part of me that hopes and prays that maybe this is all a bad dream or maybe the man I keep staring at comes out of a trance and *my* Aidan returns."

"I thought you and Val had something special."

"Val couldn't offer me anything long term. Our relationship was doomed. His first alliance was the Zops and since I'm an outcast, his race would never accept me. For the sake of his nation, Val had to let me go."

"He should've stood up for you."

My stomach twisted into a knot.

"We can debate on this forever, but the bottom line is that Val picked his race. It's over," I shrugged.

"It's gonna get better and you is gonna find someone. You see there's a silver lining waitin' for you." Jeffery patted me on my shoulder.

I smiled back. "Listen, I'll talk to Nick tonight. I'm sure we can think of some place for you and Dom to go." I reached over and hugged my dear friend.

Jeffery went back out to find Dom. I stayed back for a minute to gather my thoughts. I had so much weighing on my shoulders and there was no room for mistakes or acting impulsively. Not my best attribute.

Jeffery was a mixture of things to me, a boy-girlfriend, sometimes a mother and a father as well. Dom was straight up a father figure. And I loved them both with every last breath I had.

All the more reason why I had to separate myself from them.

Before I could make any decisions, I needed to find out what was happening outside our hideaway. It didn't take a genius to figure out that the uprising was going to get worse before there was light. My bones sensed it.

THE LAND OF YONDER

Standing at the sink in Nick's bathroom, I turned on the cool water. Thanks to his generator, we had clear running water. I splashed my face a good three times, letting the water sooth my heated skin. I didn't bother toweling. I let the water drip from my face as I paused in the mirror. I stared back at a face filled with despair and something I recognized from my past, emptiness. My throat ached with defeat. After everything I'd gone through, I stood in silence staring at a hollow face. I was lost.

What if I screw this up too? What if I let my temper get the best of me, and I acted before thinking? How many times did I have to act hastily to learn my lesson before another person died?

If I hadn't acted so foolishly and arrogantly, Dawn might still be alive today. I was faster than Mustafa. I could've outrun him. I could be holding Dawn in my arms right now, singing to her, rocking her, and reminding her everyday how much I loved her.

Suddenly, a wave of pain ripped through me and I covered my face, sobbing to the floor. I drew my knees up to my chest in a fetal position and wailed in silence.

I wasn't feeling sorry for myself. No, I didn't deserve that kind of self-indulgence. Terrible mothers didn't get to pity themselves. My daughter deserved the right to have a loving mother, one that coddles her and keeps her safe. But she didn't get that chance, and it was all because of me.

My fault.

I didn't save her. As if it was yesterday, I was standing only a few feet from her side, staring into her sweet pleading face. Dawn's angelic face would haunt me for the rest of my life. I didn't save her, and I deserved eternal punishment. I should just turn myself in to the Illuminati. Let Van do to me whatever he wished. Dom and Jeffery would be better off without me. Hell, even Nick would be better off. I brought nothing but trouble and pain to anyone who came around me.

I could end the pain right now by taking my life. No longer would I have to look in the mirror and see the face of failure. Even still, I didn't deserve taking my life. Killing myself was the easy way out. No. I deserved to suffer. I owed Dawn that much.

I didn't know how long I'd lain on the floor, but I knew if I didn't get up and make an appearance that someone would be looking for me. I didn't want anyone to catch me like this, in my moment of weakness.

I peeled myself off the floor and splashed some more water over my face, washing away any signs of tears. Even though my eyes were a little red and puffy, I hoped no one noticed.

I stepped into the small kitchen. I glanced at both guys and thought to myself that some things never changed.

Dom was working kneading bread and Jeffery sat at the small breakfast table reading an old newspaper.

"Hey, guys!" I said as I held a light note to

my voice. "Dom, can I do anything to help?" I clapped my hands together, hiding my edginess.

Both Dom and Jeffery jerked their heads up in my direction.

"I hope you had a good rest, yes?" Dom flashed a bright smile.

Jeffery's nose wrinkled as he eyeballed me. "Dom, she ain't been restin'. See those big puffy circles under her eyes?"

Oh, snap! I didn't want anyone to notice my eyes. I could strangle Jeffery. I glowered at him. "Last time I saw you, you weren't resting very much either."

Jeffery wiggled in his chair and quickly moved on to the next subject. "I'd sure been drooling over that outdoor shower. A cool shower sure would be a nice break from this unusual heat." He fanned himself with a page from of the paper. "But I don't want anyone peekin' at my lovely body. You know how shy I is." Jeffery pursed his lips, fanning the paper a little faster.

I joined him at the table. "You could wait until everyone goes to bed." An impish grin tainted the corners of my mouth. "Of course, I reckon that's when the snakes come out."

"Gurrrlfriend, watch your mouth!" Jeffery's

face drew into a frown, not missing a beat, fanning himself at near warp speed. "I knows the harshness of this yonder land. That's why I stays in the city. Now city folk, I can deal." Jeffery bobbed his head.

I smiled to myself as my attention fell on the stack of potatoes in a large basket. "Dom, I'll peel the potatoes." I rose from the table grabbing up the basket and slammed it down on the table with a jolt. I tossed Jeffery an evil eye like a pissed off sibling. Jeffery jolted, glaring at me from the rim of the newspaper. I spoke up, irately. "It wouldn't hurt for you to pitch in. I peel half and you peel the other half."

Dom turned to face me with two peelers in his hand. I took them both and then tossed the other one to my friend whose head went back to viewing the newspaper.

When the peeler hit Jeffery's chest, he yapped like a pig caught by his hindquarters. "AAaiiee!" He grabbed the peeler, cutting his eyes at me. "Gurrrlfriend, you have lost your damn mind!" Jeffery stuck his lips out, eyeing me like he wanted to throttle me.

"We all need to pull our weight around here. Those days of you sitting on your lovely caboose are over, pal." I slapped my hand on his shoulder. "We all pitch in. *Comprende*?" I arched a brow.

"Fine!" Jeffery grumbled a slew of colorful words under his breath.

Dom and I shared a laughable glance. It seemed that Jeffery might have some struggles with the new arrangements. He was going to have to toughen up a bit, get some calluses on those soft caramel colored hands of his.

I didn't mind reminding Jeff either. A little ribbing might be fun and could lighten up the mood around here. We all could use a good laugh.

On a more serious note, we needed to have a meeting of the minds and figure out an ironclad plan. What should we do with Aidan? Where to hide the guys? Should we join a militia? Could human rebels and manmade weaponry work? It was no telling what the Family had conjured up. If they had the technology to create, Sam, half-fey and creatures like me, genetically altered angels, it was anyone's guess what other monsters they might have created next.

I reckoned the first thing we needed to do was find out the advantage our enemies had and more importantly their weaknesses.

Spying was in order and time was of the essence.

There was a moment of silence as I stared out the window, slicing the peelings with more force than necessary. The sun was sinking behind the trees. Sunlight glinted off the river. Everything seemed peaceful. The river stream flowed with ease, the birds chirped gaily, the sun set. Nothing appeared affected by the collapse of this system. Regardless of how bad things seemed, the order of nature didn't change. We could learn a thing or two from nature.

I hated breaking up this pleasant moment, the three of us like it used to be, sitting around our kitchen table at the house. I inhaled a wry breath. I might not get another opportunity to speak with Dom. Regretfully, I broke the silence. "Dom, what do you think of all this craziness? Should we be afraid? We don't even know really what's going on out there." I picked up a new potato and began peeling it.

Dom inhaled a long breath, tossing a small towel over his shoulder. He continued chopping up potatoes, though, I could tell his worry weighed heavily on his mind. "I think Monsieur Nick is a better person to answer that question. After all, he served two tours in Iraq.

He's seen combat at its worst. What do I know about war? I'm merely a cook." He tossed a smile over his shoulder.

My face soured as I threw down the peeler and potato. "I'm afraid none of us are really prepared. This isn't a war of guns and bombs, man against man. We're dealing with a fight against supernatural forces. We can't even begin to speculate what's to come." I raked my fingers through my hair, roughly.

"We can't get too worked up over things we are unclear about. We will investigate what we are dealing with and then we will decide from there." Dom placed the ball of dough in a bowl and covered it. He wiped his hands on a towel and joined Jeffery and me at the table. He rested his elbows on the table and gave way to a long sigh. I knew what that meant.

"Stevie, you must prepare yourself for the unexpected. The Illuminati is looking for you. You are a threat to them. I think if we go deeper into hiding, perhaps somewhere in the bayou, you will be much safer," Dom paused. "Don't think you can fight them. You might have special powers, but they are many and you haven't a chance in hell against them. It would be like suicide. Staying out of sight is your best ammunition."

I'd never seen Dom's brown eyes so solemn. It was startling. "I don't know if Jeffery has had a chance to mention this to you, but I think it's best if you guys and I part ways." Dom started to speak up, shaking his head, but I held up my palm halting his protest. "Listen to me! Anyone near me is at risk. Look at that man out there that once was your friend." I nodded over my shoulder. "He's unrecognizable. Who knows what the Family has done to him! They have him under some sort of mind control. Who's to say they can't do the same to me." I swallowed the knot in my throat. "It's not safe being here with me."

Jeffery intervened. "As much as I hate sayin' it, she's right."

Dom shared a glance at his lifelong partner. I saw the love in his eyes as he and Jeffery paused silently for a moment. Then Dom slid his gentle eyes back to me. "I can't bare the idea of something happening to you. You are our child." Dom's voice nearly cracked.

I reached over and gathered him in the folds of my arms, clinging to him for several minutes before I pulled away. "I get you're scared. I'm scared too, but I have a better chance of staying alive than you out there on my own. I may not be able to fight off an army of freaks, but I can hold my own in most cases. I want you guys safe away from me until this uprising is under control or we find a place that we all can be together and remain safe."

Jeffery reached over and placed his hand on his partners shoulder. "I didn't want to leave Stevie at first either. I don't like it any more than you do, but I think our girl is right. We don't stand a chance if we stay. What are you gonna do to protect yourself? Beat some mofo with your bread? We hide until our girl comes for us."

I spoke up. "Dom, he's right. Neither one of you can stay here with me."

"Do you have an idea where we can go?" Dom asked.

Looking at the disquietude in Dom's eyes, I knew I'd made the right decision. It was settled. "I'm going to speak with Nick tonight. He knows the ins and outs of this strange land better than anyone," I reassured him. "I'm not going to let you guys down. I promise. You're going to be safe and so am I. We just need to be smart and levelheaded."

Dom's thin mustache stretched across his face. "I know you will do your best and that's good enough for Jeffery and me. But you stay safe even if it means we don't make it."

Jeffery shrieked! "Dom what the hell is you sayin'."

Dom glanced at Jeffery giving him the hush-your-mouth, look. Then he focused his gaze back to me. "You might be an angel, but there is only so much you can do. So… save yourself. You are so much more valuable than Jeffery and I will ever be. We are mere humans. You have gifts that can help the masses. People are going to need your help."

I sat there listening to Dom, shaking my head. "I don't want to hear that kind of talk." I grabbed his shoulders. "I'm not leaving you and Jeffery behind." I stared into his deep browns forcing the full meaning of my intent.

Jeffery interjected. "Whew! I'm glad to hear that. For a minute, I thought you meant for Stevie to leave us to hang."

"Jeffery!" Dom scolded. "We have to think of the greater good. We are not part of this grand scale. Though Stevie can't do this alone, the world still needs her if the human population is going to survive. There are millions depending on her leadership."

"Guys, please don't argue over me." I held my palms out. "I am a lab experiment. What can I offer these good folks? Feed thousands by making one fish into a meal for everyone?" I exhaled. "I throw knives. That's my gift." There was a faint tremor in my voice. Their belief in me touched me, but it terrified me even more.

"You have more to offer than you realize, chéri. Did you forget how you handled Aidan? In all the years I have known him, there has never been anything to frighten him as you did. I felt your strength. The electricity in the air was mighty powerful." Dom's soft voice touched me.

I let out a long audible breath. "My abilities are not reliable. I never know when they're going to work. Besides look what happened to me when I released my anger on Aidan. I turned into a hideous green monster." I shivered, hugging my waist.

"Now don't beat yourself up for that," Jeffery chimed in. "You weren't *that* ugly. I heard from the fat lady's society that green is the new trend."

I rolled my eyes at my friend. "Really?"

"Jeffery!" Dom snapped.

"I'm just sayin'" Jeffery shrugged.

A FEW GOOD MEN

I stepped outside onto the front porch and spotted Aidan still tied up in the same rocker. Aidan's head slightly nodded my way. His eyelids were heavy. He appeared drained and his face carried the color of agony. I didn't notice any blood lining the magick rope or his white shirt. A good indication that the rope wasn't cutting into his skin. If I didn't know any better, I'd think the druid was ill. Yet how was that possible when he was an immortal?

He started a violent bout of coughing. His face paled and his lips changed to blue. He was choking, struggling to breathe. I huffed a loud sigh and spun on my heels, heading back inside.

When I returned, I had a glass of tap water and a cloth for the blood he just coughed up. I wiped the blood that drooled from the corner of his mouth and then tilted the glass to his lips as he drank generously.

"Why are you coughing up blood? Are you sick?"

Aidan cut his heated eyes at me and then back at the glass for his second gulp. He kept drinking greedily as though he'd traveled a desert for days, deprived of water.

After he'd drained the glass, he gnarled. "I'm fine! I'm not use to inhaling all this damn dirt." His voice was sharp, but he was short winded. I slipped my eyes over him. Even under the twilight, his skin looked pallid. This was new to me.

"Since when does a little dust make you cough blood?" I eyed him suspiciously.

Aidan cut his harsh eyes back at me. "Since when do high school dropouts become doctors?"

My first impulse was to slap him. How ironic of him to say such a thing. My education was abruptly disrupted when he decided to frame me for murder. I held my tongue though and replied in a calm voice. "Since I became a serial killer." I paused holding the glass at my side, tapping it against my thigh. "You want some more water?" My voice was remote, void of emotions.

Aidan's bloodshot eyes lingered on my breasts a moment too long, and then he lifted his gaze to me. "I'm good on the water part. You offering any other services?" If I didn't know any better, this Aidan would've never treated me like a whore. I was starting to believe more and more that the Family had altered his brain.

I merely shook my head, setting the glass down on a small table beside Aidan and walked off. I didn't stomp or stalk. I simply walked away.

I was getting better at controlling my temper. Good thing too because I would've ended his life right then and there.

I hopped down the stairs and made my way over to the Cajun's side. "Hey!" I forced a smile. "It looks like we're having quite a crowd." My eyes dropped to several meat pans spread over a wooden table next to the grill. I didn't dare ask what kind of beast he'd butchered. Some things were best left alone.

With food shortages, I reckoned I best get use to eating unsavory meals.

"*Oui!* It seems that way, doesn't it?" The Cajun briefly looked up at me with a condescending grin.

I rolled my eyes. "Who's coming?" I swiped a quick glance over my shoulder at the porch where Aidan continued to sit. His gaze stayed fixed on me with a heavy dose of loathing.

"A few fellows. They are tough as nails. I think we can use their help."

I blew out a whistle. "You do know that humans don't really have much of a chance, right? Could he be that blind or was he speaking from pride? "It's gonna take superhuman powers if we're going to have a fighting chance. You don't happen to know a super-soldier militia, do you? We don't need to risk anymore lives!"

"*Oui!* I agree. These men are not your run of the mill kind of men."

"Yeah! Well, they bleed, don't they?"

"Do you bleed, *non*?" The Cajun cut his eyes at me, challenging.

"I'm not exactly like Val, a Zophasemin."

"So, what! *Si vous êtes un ange!* (if you are an angel) Like I said, do you bleed?" He looked at me with reaching eyes.

"Yes, I bleed just like any human," my jaw tightened. "I'm a synthetic angel. I was created in a lab."

"Excusez-moi!" His brow shot up. "How did they create you?"

I crinkled my forehead. "That's an interesting question. I'll have to get back to you on that one when I find out myself."

The Cajun nodded at Aidan. "Did that bastard's family have anything to do with your creation?"

I clasped my hands together, rocking on my heels. "Yep, and that's a huge problem."

"Gul, if you know something, you best spit it out." The Cajun snarled as he gathered a slab of meat in his tongs and dropped it onto the grill. Flames hissed, licking the air in protest.

I reckoned I needed to fess up, "We might have a problem. I mean, *I* may have a problem," I huffed, kicking the dirt with my boot. "The Family might be able to trace me."

His brown eyes hardened. "Why do you say that?"

"Aidan mentioned that the Family may have implanted a tracking device in me. He also claimed that when Sara sealed the contract, delivering me to Aidan, the implant had been deactivated." I shrugged. "At the time, I believed him but now," I wrinkled my nose. "I'm not sure."

The Cajun looked at me and then his gaze lifted to Aidan and then back to me. "We can't be certain much of anything right now other than we are confronting hell. We will decide as a collective. If they come, we'll be ready."

"I think we need to find the guys a place to hide and fast. Do you have any friends who live on the bayou? The deeper the better."

"Let's not do anything until we have a plan in motion. If we are being watched, we need to act as normal as possible. If their spies are watching and we do anything that might give them alarm, they might come at us with God knows what."

"Don't forget we have one of their most prized members, Aidan," I half-whispered.

"Yes, and I think he just might be our meal ticket for getting us out of this shit-bath."

"I'm not sure I follow you."

"Our prisoner could be a spy for them. He sits and listens to everything and watches our moves. You've heard that saying about keeping your enemy closer?"

"Yeah, but I don't think the person who said that was thinking of a supernatural Holocaust?"

"Don't worry about it. My men know what they are getting themselves into. We may be mere flesh and bone, with more liquor than blood, but our experience and know how makes up where we lack," he flashed an arrogant grin. "Now hand me that tray over there on the table. We need to get this *barbe à queue* cranked up."

I hated when this human tried to make light of the situation. I shoved the pan in his chest, though he didn't flinch. His pride was going to get him killed and all of us with him. He had no idea what dangers were embarking upon us. No one did.

The Cajun took the pan from me and suddenly my attention veered at the bloody slab of meat he'd dumped onto the hot charcoal. "That-that's a... !" I stammered, gaping.

"*Oui!*" the Cajun concurred. "You like gator, yes?"

"Are you *crazy*? I'm not eating that!"

The Cajun burst into a howl of laughter that could've broken the sound barrier.

"Look! This might be your usual diet, but I'm not the Wild Man of Terrebonne of the bayou. It wouldn't hurt you to give me time to adjust to your strange palate."

"You better hurry, then." His deep browns sparkled in the fire. "We may not have any other food than what is graced to us from the swamp. Did your pampered ass ever think about that?"

"What happened to fish?"

"Tsk, tsk!" he wagged his finger. "You are going to have a difficult time down here in the basin, *visage d'ange!*" (angel face)

"Don't call me that!"

"If you wish." His eyes danced with mischief. "*Très bien,* (very good) you might prefer it to other names I could call you."

"Get over yourself, Saint Nick! My advice to you is don't piss off an angel." I matched his mirthful eyes with snarky green darts.

"*Excusez-moi.* I like to tease a little too much."

"I'll go get more barbeque sauce." I wasn't in the mood for his nonsense.

When I returned outside with my arms full of bottled sauce, the whole front yard sounded like motocross speedway. The roars of motorcycles had drowned out the usual gentle hum of the cicadas. Apparently, the party had arrived as the revving bikes parked to a dusty quiet; several deep male voices meandered from the stand of trees. I quickly spotted several heads of men encircling the Cajun, giving bro hugs and popping beer bottle tops.

Standing on the top step, I glanced back at Aidan. Still battened down in the rocker, he'd nodded off to sleep. His head dropped to the side and his chest moved faintly from breathing. A pain of guilt licked through me. Maybe I should lay him down on one of the beds. Even in his sleep, his face appeared strained. We couldn't keep him in that chair all night. I needed to speak to Nick about this. Maybe he had a cot that we could put Aidan on. At least he'd be lying down.

Exhaling a deep sigh, I made my way down to the burly guest huddled in a circle.

The Cajun's head popped up. His grin flashed briefly, dazzling against his olive skin. He was in his element, obviously happy. "Come Stevie, let me introduce you to these losers," he shouted, laughing

Yep! He's in his comfort zone, alright. Men insult each other when they're buddies. A tradition that I'd never understand.

I walked up beside the Cajun and he gently placed his hand in the small of my back. I quickly stiffened. A bit taken aback, I didn't see that coming from Ole Saint Nick.

The Cajun commenced with the introductions. He slapped his hand on the stocky guy's shoulder and said, "This son of a bitch is Toe. Don't let his size fool you. Despite what he says, he can't eat a whole gator." An eruption of male laughter wafted in the air. I nodded at the man and smiled. Toe wasn't as tall as Nick, though much thicker, and packing a bulging mid-section. I wondered if the man thought his beard, long to his waist, hid his jutting belly? Like most bikers, Toe wore a leather vest at least two sizes too small with a skull on the back and tattoos that embellished his meaty arms.

The Cajun continued. "This is the one and only Dopy." The long-haired man smiled, flashing broken teeth as the Cajun clapped down on his shoulder. "This poor bastard can't hold his liquor." Guffaws followed. The men seemed to enjoy the Cajun's taunting. I gathered they were all close friends, a bond one rarely saw. I waved my hand at Dopy and smiled. He politely nodded. "Next," the Cajun moved on, "This is Titan," he snorted. "He can whoop every man in the parish except me, of course." The men roared, "But he can't whoop his old lady." The Cajun teasingly shoved his friend's baldhead. The man was a giant. He had to have been seven feet tall. Just his size and height alone could be intimidating. "That fella over there," the Cajun pointed to, "Is Slim. Now that spindly bastard *can* eat a whole gator!" Laughter poured into the air once more. The Cajun moved on to the following, "Last, but not least." He moved to the last man, standing on the outs. "That there is Scrubby with a goatee. It's safe to say he came from a long line of sheep!"

The laughter floated into the night air as I spoke up. "It's nice to meet y'all," I smiled, giving a light nod. My hands were stuffed in my pockets, uncertain if I should shake hands or slap 'em on their backs. I decided to keep my hands in my pockets.

My gaze drifted off to where several bikes with sparkling chrome sat parked. Harleys, as far as I could tell. That was a sure sign that these men were proficient bikers. Setting aside their scary appearances, they all seemed harmless enough. They were strange looking with nose piercings, tattoos and hair longer than mine. I didn't mind. I felt right at home among them.

Though, I worried how they might receive

Dom and Jeffery. I hoped Jeffery would hold his tongue. I didn't want to think what he might ask one of these grungy men.

The Cajun spoke up, "These men and I go back a few years. We are former military. Special Operations. Army soldiers."

"Wow! That's impressive," I smiled approvingly.

"These men are my brothers," Nick spoke proudly.

"Where were you men stationed?" I asked.

The Cajun slipped a sideways glance at the men and said, "Afghanistan. I was the baby of this ugly bunch! They hated me at first, cuz I was prettier."

Shrubby interjected, "Yeah! You might have been the prettiest, but you were the stupidest little wiener."

"Don't worry about my *wiener*! I save that for the ladies."

"That's not what I heard," said Titan. "Some of those gals were disappointed."

"*Non!* They wanted more of me and I turned them away. Of course, they are going to bitch. If you'd had me, you'd want more of me too." The Cajun wore pomposity like his Sunday church clothes.

Titan flashed a wide smile. "Nah! You ain't

my type. I hate whiskers on *women*." Laughter encircled the men like a domino effect. I found myself laughing too. The Cajun snorted and didn't have much of a comeback after that shade. Come to think about it, he had looked a bit peaked. I imagined only few could taunt him about his manhood.

Later that night the whole gang and I had settled around the blazing campfire, eating gator. Surprisingly, it was tasty. I found it had a lingering taste between catfish and chicken. I didn't even need the barbeque sauce. *Go figure!*

After we finished our meal, talk started to rumble. My ears were perked and ready to hear the latest events that had transpired since we took underground. I felt cut off from civilization, like a blind person standing on a cliff. I needed a heavy scoop to remedy the bothersome tick that twisted my gut.

Toe began the conversation. "I've been snooping around. Asking my peeps what they know about our city. Man, I have to tell you, it's pretty fucking bleak."

I jumped in, "What's happening?"

"To start, the United Nations has been

seized and the Order has declared martial law. This ain't just local. It's worldwide. Curfew is enforced. Anyone outside roaming the streets after eight p.m. will be gunned down. No questions asked. My informant said two neighbors of his got shot down in cold blood. They got caught pillaging through a busted-up grocery store for food. One fellow was looking for baby formula."

"Damn! Can we help these families?" The Cajun's voice was tight with anger.

"I don't know. There's regulators at every corner."

"Regulators?" Titan asked.

"Yeah, they are some strange looking fellows what I've heard. They're the enforcers of peace. Some cold-blooded bastards, I hear."

The Cajun interjected. "Are they military forces?"

Toe squinted his face like he'd eaten something rotten. "I hadn't seen 'em, but my sources say they sound like robots but look like reptiles, scales, and all. They ain't human. The street has it that they are alien. Spaceships and shit. They come from Bellatrix." He tipped his head back and pointed to the sky at a yellow star. "You can't see it all the time, but tonight the planet's brighter than normal. I looked through my telescope earlier today and you can see small streaks coming from it. My redneck guess is that they're coming in their ships. Mostly thousands headed to earth."

Curses spewed among the men.

"What has your source seen?" The Cajun asked, rubbing his bristled jaw.

"For starters, those fuckers," Toe nodded at me, "Pardon my language ma'am."

I caught Toe's gaze, "It's fine. Go on, please," I wanted to hear as much as anyone.

Toe continued. "The creatures move faster than any human. Hell, my source saw one jump a building like superman. Only this creature wasn't pretty or friendly. He threw a man off the top of a building, killing the poor man." The tensing of Toe's jaw betrayed his trepidation. "I tell you, man, my source doesn't get scared that easily. But the white in his eyes were far too wide when he finished his story. Those regulators had him spooked!"

The look on Toe's face gave me shivers. No doubt, we were all in over our heads. And the worst part, I had the feeling we'd just grazed the surface.

"Merde!" The Cajun blurted out. "What else do you know?"

"It ain't good for us po-boys." Fear laced

Toe's voice. "The uprising has shut the city down. Everything is closed banks, grocery stores, any thriving business. Even the bars have closed. The streets are filled with hungry people and dead bodies with their guts hanging out as they bleed out onto the street.

"What? Is the government pulling a Hitler regime on us?" Titan asked.

"I suspected the same thing myself, *man!*" Toe resumed. "Word is going around that our old system has fully collapsed. Riots have been going on downtown. In fact, the whole world is a massacre." He gave pause, rubbing his eyes briefly. I reckoned he was trying to keep from losing it. After a bucket of minutes, he lifted his gaze back at us and finished. "Hell, its history repeating itself. Hitler and Castro forcing working folks from their homes. It's just a matter of time before they come take our land too." Toe shook his head. The blunt of shock, fear for an uncertain future hung on his burdened shoulders.

The Cajun butted in. "It sounds like a Marxism–Leninism socialism. They intend to convert our country into a one-party socialist, under Communist Party rule. These animals seek dominance, a one government over the people. Strip folks of their possessions. Force people to surrender and follow the bastards just for food." The Cajun summed it up in a nutshell.

"These new authorities are fucking cowards. Too afraid to show their ugly mugs." Toe's whole demeanor boiled with raw anger.

"Seriously?" I clamored in shock.

The Cajun broke in, "Sorry, Red. Looks like your poor again." He had flopped his unwanted butt down beside me.

I just smiled. "Money isn't important to me. Besides, I'm glad to be rid of it. It was blood money."

The Cajun reached over and squeezed my hand. "I'm sorry. Bad joke, *yes*?

I replied. "Yes, very!" I caught a quick glimpse of regret behind his dark browns. I nudged Nick with my shoulder to make light. I didn't have the tenacity to keep up with his tough jabs. My head felt weighed down with sand. I couldn't wrap my head around the reality of my surroundings. The world was changing, and it was scaring the hell out of me.

"How are folks getting food?" The Cajun asked Toe.

"Funny, you should ask. People are forced to stand in long lines, hours at a time. In order to receive food, you have to get inked on your wrist like a tattoo. You can only detect it with a special monitor." Toe went on to say. "You won't believe what the number is, *man*." Toe shook his head, clearly shaken.

"I'm not sure I want to know." Dread swirled in the Cajun's voice.

With no warning, sleeping beauty had awaken. Aidan bellowed. "Let me guess! Would it happen to be the numbers six six six?"

"What do those numbers mean?" I asked, though, I knew it wasn't anything good.

"It stands for man's reign has come to an end. It divides the imperfect humans from the supreme humans. Imperfect man. The stamp contains a tracking device. It's how the NWO keeps track of citizens." Aidan seemed to have regained some of his steam as he leaned back in his chair, gloating.

Slim called out among the stir. "What the hell is NWO?"

With a heavy sigh, I answered, "New World Order." I cut my ireful eyes at Aidan and then back at Slim, "It's a conspiracy. The Illuminati have been planning this for centuries."

The Cajun cut in, "Slim, they're the bastards that are behind the curtain," the Cajun grated. "They're like those radicals in Afghanistan tying bombs to children. Those *sac à foutre* (scum-bags) can fuck off!

I spoke up before World War III started in Nick's front yard. "I think we need to keep our calm. We have someone who can give in-depth details of what's happening." Everyone followed the line of my gaze.

"Yeah, but will he tell the truth?" Toe stared menacingly at Aidan.

With this different Aidan, it was hard to say. "What do we have to lose?" I dragged in a biting breath.

DEED OF TRUST

By the blood-curling screams of Jeffery, I'd thought someone had skinned him alive. How that man lived in New Orleans all his life and never had eaten gator, would baffle my mind forever. That was like a Texan never eating deer. I think Jeffery was in his own genre.

A sudden dead silence fell over the crackling fire as all eyes snapped up at my good friend. Shortly following, there was a chorus of laughter. Obviously, Jeffery made a big hit with the bikers as they enjoyed a friendly slap across his boney back.

Jeffery pursed his lips and held his head high as he walked prissily over and sat down next to Dom and me without so much as an utter.

Slim nodded over to Aidan as he directed his question to me. "Since you think it's a shot… ask that fella what he knows. If he won't talk, we have ways of making him." In his deep baritone voice there was a minatory tint.

My gaze jolted sharply at Slim. I might not like my hostage, but for some reason, I felt protective of him. I wasn't ready to let any of these bikers work him over. I remembered when Aidan could've taken any one of these men and not bat an eye. Now, by the ragged look on his face, I wasn't so sure. Even still, I didn't want to find out if Aidan could hold his own. I needed to keep the peace.

Before I answered Slim, Aidan erupted. "Ask me!" he bellowed. "No need for torture." His conceit grated me. "I'll tell you anything you want to know. First, I want some food and an ice-cold beer before I divulge any information."

"I'll fix him a plate." Dom exhaled as he started to his feet.

I placed my hand on his shoulder. "Dom, no. Let me take care of Aidan. He's too unpredictable and dangerous."

After I stacked the plate full of gator and

potatoes, I swiped a cold beer from the ice barrel and marched up the steps.

Standing directly in front of him, our eyes met. His eyes were flat, hard and passionless. I knew this was going to be tricky. I had to stand my ground. I slightly shifted in my feet. "You go first, my friend. No negotiating." I stood, chin tilted slightly upward.

Aidan fumed for a second as his eyes locked into a gun-down stare at me. "Ah, she commands!"

"Cough it up!" My patience was running thin.

A smirk curved the corner of his mouth, "There's really not a lot to tell. The almighty Illuminati have destroyed the old system as you have some idea already. However, this uprising will make Hitler look like a saint. First, those deemed contaminated will be extinguished." He snarled.

"What do you mean extinguished?" I asked.

Aidan lifted his red eyes at me and smirked. "I understand why you didn't finish school. Don't you know that history repeats itself?" He then cut his eyes at the men and rose his voice. "People who do not honor the Omniscient God, the true leader, the Illuminati, and denounce their useless religions will be executed. They can meet their delightful maker who doesn't give two shits that they are suffering.

I took a step back. I was shocked over his words. "You can't expect people to lay down and surrender to your Order. They will rebel as I recall history accounts." My hands began to tremble. He was talking about mass destruction.

Aidan turned his disdainful eyes at me. "You'd be surprise what a person will do for a little food and a warm place to sleep."

I gawked at him as my stomach churned. I looked down at the plate of food and the cold beer in my hand. "Strange that you should say that." I nodded over my shoulder to the men. "You brazenly brag to these good folks about starving people to get them to bend to your will and yet these folks are willing to feed you for just a little information." My lips curled into a scowl. "Go screw yourself!" I threw the food over the rail. "I'm tired of your bullshit!" I spun on my heels and headed inside the house. I'd had my limit with Aidan, but I had to finish hearing what else he had to say. I halted in the doorframe listening.

"Your friend is correct." He nodded to Toe. "The government has declared a state of emergency. If you resist, and you will, the regulators will shoot dissenters on sight. You're defiant. And you will not conform to the *New World Order*. You are the bottom of the barrel and are only good for slaves."

The men began to stir restlessly. Murmurs of curses wafted in the night air.

I flinched when the word slave came out of his mouth. I could only imagine what he meant. The only explanation I could see was that the Family had Aidan under mind control. What else could it possibly be? I swallowed down the pending dread and asked, "The regulators are the police now."

"Yes," Aidan went on to explain, "They are the new law enforcement. All citizens must be contained to keep the peace."

"What do you mean contained." My neck bristled.

"The regulators are ordered to do whatever it takes to keep the populace calm. Anyone who is opposed to our cause will be shot down in plain sight."

The Cajun scoffed. "I suppose killing innocent women and children is keeping the peace."

A hunted look came over Aidan's face. "The

Order will do whatever it takes to keep the compliance."

"So, we don't get a vote?" the Cajun asked.

Aidan laughed. "Of course not! The Order is not a utopian society. Freedom will be stripped from every living soul."

The Cajun stood up, stalking his way to the porch. He stopped at the bottom steps.

A breath of relief eased from my chest. I was glad the Cajun didn't come any closer. Aidan, with a mere thought, could've snapped the Cajun in two. I didn't want to have to step between a 300-year-old-druid and a big-headed human.

"You do realize the old leaders and the people will rebel. You're asking for war." The Cajun's voice came off tight and ready to blow up with rage.

Aidan sneered. "Neither the officials in the White House, including the president, nor the CIA, FBI, or even the NSA, have ever actually been in charge. That's why it has been a breeze taking over. The old system you once knew no longer exists. Out with the old and in with the new."

"Are you saying other countries are under siege?" By the twitching of the Cajun's jaw I could tell he wanted to pounce on Aidan.

"That is correct." An insidious grin abraded Aidan's face. "We, the Illuminist are the supremacy. We are the only hope you have. Not your weak government nor the UN can help you now. It is *we* who have ceased all wars. Soon we will claim peace and security. Only those who subject themselves to our authority will reap the benefits of our pardon."

The words fell out of my mouth before I could stop myself. "What happens if we resist?"

"Freedom Fighters will die," he paused with a scowl welded to his face. "For you, sweetheart, your days are numbered regardless."

With no warning, my eyes ignited as a faint gasp settled among the men. "What do you *mean*?" I asked as I stepped onto the porch, forgetting that the men didn't know about my druid gifts. I wasn't sure how I'd explain this either. It was a gift I'd inherited from Aidan when we'd sealed our fate as one. Funny, I had yet to have seen Aidan's eyes flame. I wondered if I'd taken the ability from him.

"Do you think they are just going to let you get off scot free?" Aidan didn't wait for me to respond. "My uncle, our Grandmaster, is determined to have your head on a silver platter. He has ordered for you to be hunted down and destroyed. He claims you are a danger to the New World Order. You must be eliminated."

My mouth flew open. "Oh, really! They're going to have a tough time bringing me down, buddy!" I promised with fist to my side, white knuckled.

"I didn't assume otherwise," Aidan scoffed. "Don't you think they have prepared for your little bag of tricks?"

"Speaking of tricks..." My eyes narrowed with suspicion. "Where are yours?"

Aidan's body tightened. "When I'm drained of energy, my powers are depleted," he snarled.

"Is that why you're spitting up blood?"

"I haven't spit up any blood," he lied.

I gawked at him for a minute and then with a heavy sigh, I replied, "You're lying, but if you want to save face, that's fine. I don't care if you're coughing up your dick!" An explosion of laughter burst into the night's dew. I was sure that I'd scored a few points for that jab.

"You really should be more concerned for yourself," Aidan gravely advised.

"What are you saying?"

"You don't know, do you?" His laugh assaulted my ears.

"I wouldn't have asked if I knew."

"Well, let me enlighten you, sweetheart," he paused flashing his smile. Was I imagining things or was Aidan's teeth starting to decay? Perhaps his druid years were catching up to him. I pulled my eyes from his smirk and crossed my arms over my chest.

"Thanks to your DNA, they have cloned an army of soldiers with your same novel capabilities," Aidan continued. "You have multiple blood relatives. We refer to you as the new age Eve. Though for you, it will be a short celebration. I'm expecting your family reunion will be a huge bang!"

"Have you gone mad?" I knew with certainty this was the beginning of the end. Aidan confirmed my suspicions. I was a liability. Anyone around me would face the same fate. *Holy crap!* I ripped my fingers through my tangled hair. We were doomed. I slid my gaze at the Cajun. When our eyes latched, I instantly knew he realized the peril we were in.

Then, Aidan distracted me from my nightmarish thoughts. "Your friend is right. The Order has eminent domain. The change will be a feudal society. A military hierarchy in which the ruler will have control and say over the land. Only those worthy of such a privilege to possess land will receive deeds of trust. However, the Order has the right to revoke the tenant's ownership and kick his ass to the streets if he breaks the *Order of Solomon.*

The Cajun's eyes flashed a grave look at our captive. "I'm sick of hearing this Euro's trash talk! Too much talk." The Cajun darted up the steps heading toward Aidan.

Since I'd made the druid my responsibility, I stepped in front of the Cajun. He grasped my arms and lifted me to the side. *"Non!"* he barked. "Let one of the men get him."

"Fine!" I stepped back, palms in the air.

The Cajun nodded to Titan.

Moments later, Aidan found himself face down in the dirt in the center of a circle of men. He was nearly kissing the Cajun's boots.

My magical rope still clung to Aidan's body, but it didn't stop him from rising on his haunches as he raked his baleful eyes over the circle of bikers as if he were memorizing their faces.

I cringed, fearing for their lives. These humans were tough, but I feared if Aidan had only a mere smudge of his powers, they wouldn't stand a chance.

When my eyes gravitated to the Cajun's

face, my breath stalled. His taunt expression reminded me of a lion inching closer to its kill. "Start talking or else I'll cut your tongue out, yes?"

For a minute, I pitied Aidan. He looked beaten like a dog kicked to submission, but he still had some fight in him as he spoke with audacious pride. "My family is many." Aidan's voice was raspy as sandpaper. "We have a far reach beyond what your pathetic minds can grasp. This planet is only a speck of our scope compared to the range of our supremacy. We are in the folds of profound change and not one of you simpletons can appreciate the magnitude and benefits of our rising."

"I have a mind to run the girl's dagger through your black heart right now!" The Cajun's jaw was set in steel.

Aidan broke into laughter that seeped of venom. "Watch what you threaten, lowly one. I can take every one of you in one swift sweep."

If Aidan's threat had worried the Cajun, he didn't show it. Rather, he went on with his interrogation. "*Vous ne me fais pas peur avec votre visage dans la boue.*" (You do not frighten me with your face in the dirt.) The Cajun grated. "Tell me why your people want the girl."

"Why do you care? She's a useless whore!" The acidity in his voice was prolific.

The Cajun interrupted with little tolerance. "Don't talk about the girl that way. After all, she was the mother of your child. Get on with what you know. And make it quick before I lose my patience."

Aidan flashed a fiendish sneer. "A little scared there, human?" He carefully shifted on his knees as he glared at the different faces staring down at him, "You are fools if you take this lightly," he bellowed. "If you are willing to set aside your differences, The Order will pardon your crimes. Join in our takeover and pledge your allegiance to the New World Order. I will see to it that you are each given a unit of land in exchange for your military services. Nothing short will be acceptable. Failure to do so will result in death."

I couldn't listen to his vile any longer. I stormed down the steps and pushed my way through a couple of men until I reached Aidan's side. I spoke out against his fanatical babble. "You're describing a monopoly, but really in truth, we will be slaves to your damn family." I raked in a shard of breath and knocked Aidan down into the dirt, face grinding against the ground. I dug my foot into the nemesis's back. "You mentioned an army like me. *Elaborate!*" I gritted my teeth.

"Since you were not in compliance with the Family, we went to plan B."

"Plan B?" I hesitated briefly, then it hit me. I flung into action, flipping him on his back. "You son of a *bitch!*" I throttled him, pressing my dagger to his throat. The Cajun caught me by my waist, pulling me back as I barely missed Aidan's jugular. Still, I fought to get at him. "You gave our daughter over to that beast, Mustafa. And in return, that monster gave you his DNA!" The Cajun had a death grip on me. "Forget this shit!" I ordered my dagger to ram through his collarbone. I heard bone snap and immediately following, Aidan howled. The next knife loomed evenly at his eye level. "You are nothing but a black hearted *monster!*" I spat in his face.

Aidan's grin transformed into something unrecognizable. Pure evil, I speculated. "I am a survivor, my dear. I follow orders and I stay alive. Hate me if you wish. Where I stand, I have no choice. The Order wanted your DNA. For the exchange of your daddy, Mustafa's DNA, we bargained with the child," he gnarled. "If you ask me, we got the better deal."

All this time, Aidan had looked me straight in the eye and lied to me. He was in on the plan with Mustafa all along.

Unable to contain myself, I snapped. Blinded by rage, I dove for Aidan. But before I had a chance to squeeze my fingers around his throat, I felt a sudden sharp force to the back of my head and all at once, everything went blank.

FREEDOM FIGHTERS

The morning came as a thin beam of light hit me straight in the face. I slowly opened my eyes. With my head full of cobwebs, I skimmed the surroundings and my memory came flooding back. A throbbing ache resonated from the crown of my head. My fingers grazed the spot but I flinched, regretting my move. It stung like a *mother*. I had a good hunch the huge goose bump on my noggin came from a blunt object. And the force behind the strike could only have been one person... *the Cajun.*

"Ouch!" I mumbled. "Damn that hurts!" Did he have to hit me so hard? I get why he needed to stop me. We needed to keep the prisoner alive. I couldn't believe I almost killed Aidan. He was our only connection to *the Family*.

Whata nightmare! We were helpless. Innocent people were going to die. And those sociopaths didn't care. Self-entitled *pricks*! I covered my arm over my eyes, trying to will my mind to go blank. Yet old memories gnawed at me. I remembered a time that seemed so long ago. A time when Aidan stayed by my side to comfort me. A tear escaped and I quickly wiped it away with the back of my hand. I missed *that* Aidan. The one who saved me many times from the harsh fate of death. Even the underhanded things he had done seemed tenable. But now, not a glimmer of the old Aidan I once knew. I wondered if *that* Aidan had ever existed? Whether or not he was a figment of my imagination, he felt real to me. How I craved to feel his arms around me. I still ached for our child. My child that I'd never been able to cradle in my arms. I knew wishing wasn't going to bring Dawn back or the man I once loved. I had to focus on surviving in the present. A daunting task I feared.

I worried over the Cajun and his men. Even though they had fought in a gruesome war, it didn't prepare the men for this catastrophe. They should lay low, live off the swamp.

To add to the heap of woes, I worried about Jeffery and Dom. They wouldn't make it in the wild. They were accustomed to a pampered lifestyle. They had no survival skills. Maybe, the men could teach Dom and Jeff some survival skills. That might not be a bad idea, but did we have enough time? After all, it was only a matter of time before the Illuminist found us.

Val came to mind and a spurt of anger smacked me like a coconut dropping from a tree. Why did he leave us to fight this battle alone? How could I fend off these monsters with no proficient back up? Humans were defenseless against the Illuminist's army of super-freaks. I needed angel power. If there was a fleet of genetically engineered angels coming for me... how the hell was I to fight them off? An impossible endeavor.

I couldn't lie here all day and do nothing. I needed to speak with Nick.

I threw the covers off and gently swung my legs off the bed to the floor. I sat for a moment letting my head stop spinning. I inhaled a few heavy breaths to ease the pain and settle my stomach. As my sickness lessened, I scanned the room for my clothes. I had only my tank top and panties on. I didn't even want to think who undressed me. I had enough on my plate as it was already. This one, I'd let slid. I spotted some clothes laid out over a chair in the corner. I raised off the bed and padded over to the folded clothing. I'd never seen these threads before. It was army combat gear. A cap, khaki pants, tee shirt, a black sports bra, go figure on that one. And boots my size. I grabbed up the pants and they were my size too. I guess these items were meant for me. I tied my hair up in a ponytail with a band I'd found on the nightstand. Then I covered my hair up with the cap, letting my ponytail hang out. I stood in front of the mirror. Not too bad, I thought as I eyed myself carefully.

Moments later, I stepped outside and noted right away that the boys had moved Aidan to the large oak tree just off to the side of the porch. My breath eased when I spotted the magick rope still intact, wrapped around him like a tight rubber band.

Aidan and I swapped glances and neither one of us bothered with pleasantries. I think after last night, we'd exchanged enough insults to last a lifetime.

I combed my eyes over the grounds.

Everything had settled. I saw no signs of the bikers. They must've left last night after I got knocked out. The sun was climbing the blue sky and the heat was following quickly after.

Judging by the high sun, the morning was almost over. I quickly spied the Cajun making a bunch of ruckus inside his storage building, set high off the ground like the house. I made my way to him, climbing the steps. When I stepped inside, my eyes instantly landed on a metal table stock-piled of guns and grenades. The Cajun was dismantling his rifle. I cleared my throat. "Good morning."

Nick turned to me, combing his eyes over me. "You gotta good bump on the head there, yes?"

"Yeah," I half scoffed. "Did you have to hit me so hard?" My fingers touched my forehead and I flinched.

"When you act *coo-yon*, I do what I must." The corner of his lip twitched.

"Coo-yon? I'm far from foolish." I could feel the onset of irritation starting to sizzle.

"Maybe, maybe not. But I can't have you ruining the only leverage we have." He nodded at Aidan. "Without pretty boy, our ass is cooked." The Cajun's dark eyes collided with Aidan's withering stare.

I decided to change the subject as my eyes swiped over all his arsenal goodies spread about over the table in a nice neat line. "Wow! Looks like you've been stocking up for a while. Is it legal to carry this much weaponry?" I thought David Koresh, a notorious cult leader in Waco, Texas a few years back, had some serious ammo, but the Cajun puts that dude to shame.

He nodded toward the back of the building. "Go see for yourself."

When I reached the back, my chin hit the floor. I whistled, "Damn! You have a serious hobby!" It quickly came to mind the collection of weapons that Val stored in his gym. They were more magical than manmade but very effective.

"Is it even legal for you to carry so much arms?" I slipped a sideways glance at the Cajun and then back at the rows of tubs full of every kind of gun one could possibly imagine.

"At one time, it was illegal. Now, I don't give a shit. I fight for my rights. That's the only law I honor."

The conviction in the Cajun's voice was impregnable. To be honest, I agreed. Yet I feared he might be fighting a lost cause. You didn't bring a knife to a gunfight. His collection of weaponry might be quite destructive to the norm, but I had a sneaky feeling it was nothing more than a water gun up against the Order's artillery.

As I made my way back to the Cajun's side, my stomach twisted in knots. I had to get this man to understand that his weapons were useless. "If Aidan is right, those soldiers are super-soldiers. You think mankind's arsenals will serve your purpose?" I didn't want to douse the Cajun with despair, but I had to be real.

"Nope! I don't." The Cajun answered while he cocked one of his rifles back and looked down its barrel. I stared at him baffled.

"Then what's the point?"

The Cajun finally glanced up at me. "It might not kill 'em but it might slow them down long enough for us to get away."

He went back to cleaning his gun.

I stood there chewing the inside of my mouth. Then a thought popped up. "Homemade bombs might be more effective."

The Cajun snapped his head up, glaring at me like I was 'Jihadi John'. "What's going on inside that pretty head of yours?"

"I'm just saying… if these creatures are not

of this world, they may be sensitive to certain human products."

Out of nowhere, Aidan burst into cackles.

The Cajun's eyes blazed with murder. "What's so funny, druid?"

"Nothing will defeat our super-soldiers. Freedom fighters!" Aidan crowed.

"You over there shut your trap! Unless you want to eat turpentine." By the scorn on the Cajun's face, I gathered that he wasn't making an idol threat.

Strangely, Aidan regarded bitterly, simmering to a quiet. The old Aidan would have never backed down.

The Cajun cut his eyes back to me. "Exactly what do you have in mind?" He kept his voice just above a whisper.

I whispered back. "Like common household items."

"*Non!*" he shook his head. "We can't test it on any of those bastards. We'll be wasting our time." He returned to his gun cleaning.

I bit my bottom lip, thinking. "Hmm, you can use me." I shrugged. "Who else would be a better lab rat?" I feigned a smile.

That was the first time I'd seen the look of shock on the Cajun's face. "Come again?"

"Well, someone has to test the product. The only way we're going to find out if the chemicals work is testing them on me. We don't have to use a full dose." I stood there silent while the Cajun stared at me as if I'd lost my mind. Maybe I had. Still the same, what other choice did we have?

All of a sudden, he uttered a slew of curse words, "Gul, what is wrong with you?"

"You got any better ideas?" I stood at an impasse with my arms folded with a lock down stare at the Cajun.

He rubbed his two-day-old stubble. "What kind of homemade bombs are you talking about?"

"If we used household goods, we'd have ourselves an arsenal of bombs far more effective than your most mighty guns." I nodded at the trash bin and under the house, "All these beer bottles and any plastic bottles laying around, will come in handy. Got any balloons?" I crossed my arms, staring the Cajun dead in the eye.

"You're not kidding, are you?"

"Nope, but it can get tricky. If you shake 'em they can explode."

"How do you know these things?" The Cajun's eyes glazed with shock.

A wicked grin skirted across my face, "I paid attention in chemistry."

The Cajun paused with a look of death on his face, and then suddenly he blurted out, "*Non!* I don't think so!"

"Look we can use a little on a small spot of skin." I rolled my sleeve up showing bare skin.

"*Non!* It could be fatal."

The man was more stubborn than a barnyard of mules, but I couldn't back down now. "If it kills me, then we know it works." I glared back at him, hell-bent.

"You are *couyon* (crazy), yes?"

"Yes." I said flat, staring into his black opal eyes.

He stomped his foot and raked his fingers through his disheveled hair. "*Assez!*" (Enough) He let out a huff in his heavy French accent. "Only a drop on your skin. You got that, gul?"

"*Oui*, Saint Nick!" I snapped my heels together and saluted sharply with a broad smiled.

"Grrrr," the Cajun rumbled. "Don't use my name until you survive the test. I hate being on first name basis with someone on her deathbed," he grumbled.

～

Eight hours later and I looked like someone who stepped into a hornet's nest. The welts were red and full of pus. Although, it was painful, we now had bombs that might take down a few super-soldiers.

No matter how pretty the sun looked dipping behind the horizon, another concern picked at my gut. How would we identify the super ones from a regular human? They could look like anyone on the street, blending into the crowd. It was going to be tough dividing the humans from the unhuman. Unless they wore a stamp across their forehead, we were going to have to take our chances. That meant we were going to have to be alert of every person out in the open and even those lurking in the shadows. I raked in a fretful sigh. The odds were against us and yet we still stood to fight. Freedom fighters or suicide idiots?

BOMBS AWAY

"*J*effery, I understand that you're afraid." He followed closely behind me into the kitchen like a puppy dog. I tossed over my shoulder as I headed for the coffee pot. "Despite the risk, I have to do this." I grabbed a cup from the cupboard and poured myself a cup of coffee. I took a seat at the small table by the window as Jeffery stayed on my heels. I sighed, thinking what I'd give for a little sugar and cream. "Don't worry." I lifted my gaze at my pestering friend. "I'll be with the Cajun," I shrugged. "We have to see what's out there."

"Let Nick and one of his buddies go scope out the city! For once in your life let the men take the lead." Jeffery raved, standing over me with determination etched in his sour face.

"My friend," I reached up, grasping my fingers around his hand, "I appreciate your concern, but this is what I was made to do. I'm just like one of those super-soldiers. I'll be okay. Stop worrying your beautiful head over me."

"My beautiful head and all my other lovely *isn't the point!*" Jeffery's voice went up an octave.

I blew out an irate sigh. "I can hold my own with the best." I wasn't wavering on my decision.

"One on one, gurrrl! Not no hundred clones like yourself. You go out there it'll be like walkin' out naked to a firing squad." I stifled a giggle. Only Jeffery could use nudity in a situation daring as this.

I'd placed the guys in a dangerous position by mere association. For that reason alone, I needed to step up to the plate and protect them. That meant I needed to see what was going on in the city. I might not know combat, but common sense told me that before any of us could make any strategic move, we needed to see for ourselves what was going on.

I gulped my hot coffee down, feeling the sear down my windpipe. I didn't care. I needed its boost last week. I didn't have it in me to argue with a damn grasshopper, much less Jeffery. "Look!" I sighed deeply. "I don't have the answer for everything. We have to go into the city and check out what's happening. I might be able to speak to some of the locals. Maybe they can give us some insight." I took another gulp of coffee, somehow the burn kept my mind from going AWOL.

Dom came into the kitchen greeting us with a tired smile. *"Bonjour!"* he started shuffling through the cabinets and fridge to see what to fix for his usual morning breakfast.

Jeffery and I both mumbled, "Morning," in a half-hearted way. Neither one of us were in the best mood.

Though considering our current dilemma, we were in pretty good shape. Fortunately, Toe had been kind enough to bring us a few dozen eggs and he'd butchered a nutria, a bayou rabbit. At least we'll be eating, even if the food was less than desirable.

When I first laid eyes on that furry varmint, I nearly choked. I swore it was an over-sized rat. Yet in this strange land of Louisiana, I found myself often surprised.

After Dom had skinned it and made it into chili, it turned out quite tasty. Of course, Dom could make anything taste good. To add to the list of worry, with little food supply, we might be eating a lot more of those critters. The bayou had plenty of nutria to keep us fed. On top of that, the fur might be good for trade.

Soon Dom busied himself with breakfast. It didn't take Dom long before he began rolling out dough, making his simple rolls. I hoped he planned to make some gravy from the milk that Slim brought us, fresh from his cow. Dom showed me how to make butter from the cream. I reckoned in times like this, having a little know how of nature was a priceless tool to have in your back-pocket. It could be a matter of life and death.

Jeffery decided to bring Dom into our lovely discussion. "Do you think it's safe enough for Stevie to go into the city while Aidan's family's lookin' for her? She's gonna get her head chopped off."

"I think it is dangerous for all of us," Dom sighed. "Unfortunately, it might be a necessary risk."

"See! he agrees!" I stuck my tongue out at Jeffery like an annoying sibling.

"Gurrrlfriend, don't get your panties in a bunch just yet. He might change his mind when he finds out what you plan to do!"

Jeffery pursed his lips and straightened his shoulders back, snapping his fingers in my face.

"Children!" Dom scolded. "Stop!"

Jeffery chimed in. "She's gonna throw homemade bombs at those mofo monsters!"

"I'm not going right up to a regulator and yell… hey, nana, nana, boo, boo, you can't catch me!" I sang, pushing Jeffery's buttons.

"Gurrrl, you ain't too big to slap!" Jeffery twisted his lips into a snarl.

"Stop worrying! We plan to blend in with the crowd. We're merely going to observe. That's all. I swear!" I slapped Jeffery on the back and flashed a grin.

"Then why is Aidan's Jeep gettin' loaded down with homemade bombs?" Jeffery crossed his arms, bobbing his head like the cat that ate the canary.

"*What*?" I sprung from my chair and darted out the front door and made a beeline to where the Cajun and Titan were gathered.

Once I reached their side, I stopped, gaping at Aidan's Jeep. They'd taken the top off and were making more than minor changes to the car. "What are you doing?" I washed my eyes over the once bright yellow Jeep and cut my gaze at the Cajun and Titan. "The Jeep looks like green vomit." I walked around the car, inspecting. "How did all these dings get here? Even the front bumper is banged up and twisted." The Frenchman ignored me as he moved to the back of the Jeep, squatting down with a screwdriver in his hand. I stalked over to his side. "This car looks like crap!"

The Cajun cut his eyes at me briefly, answering curtly. "*Oui!*"

"And may I ask why?" I glimpsed over at Aidan shooting blue shards my way. I reckoned he didn't appreciate the minor adjustments to his Jeep either.

Titan spoke up. "We can't drive around with a brand-new Jeep that's bright yellow and with the same license plate. They'd see us coming."

"After you've smashed it, this thing doesn't look like it'll get us out of the driveway." I noticed a sledgehammer laying in the dirt.

"That's the point!" Titan grinned underneath his gruffly beard. We'll look like po-folks beggin' for handouts."

After changing the plates, the Cajun came around the car to Titan and me. He raked his eyes over me like he was summing me up like I was the new dog to the pack. "You need to dirty up a bit. It wouldn't hurt to tear some holes in your shirt and pants." He studied my hair, fingering a strand in his fingers. "Keep that cap on. Your red hair is distracting."

"Whatever!" I slapped his hand way. "What about the bombs? I noticed you got 'em loaded."

"*Peut être.* (Maybe)" The Cajun flashed a mischievous grin.

"Holy hell! I didn't intend for you to use those unless we were under attack," I gawked at the two men who seemed far too confident.

The Cajun stepped up, looming over me. "We're headed into hostile territory. I'm not taking any chances."

Titan spoke up. "It's best to expect the unexpected, Ms. Stevie."

I glimpsed at the back of the Jeep. I spotted several crates that were used to contain mudbugs or crabs. "Why crates?" I went to move a lid and the Cajun snatched my hand back.

"*Non,* gul!" he said sternly. "Don't open those crates unless you intend to lose a finger."

"What's in there?"

The Cajun snarled with pride. "We put snappers in the crates in case we get searched."

A smile tugged on the corners of my mouth. "Aren't you full of surprises!" I didn't think about disguising the weapons. Such a clever idea, but I hoped they didn't think I was throwing the bombs.

"We aren't as green behind the ears as you think," the Cajun smiled brightly. War seemed to suit him as if he thrived on it.

Then our pending reality struck. "Fools, you are!" Aidan yelled out. "When they have you blindfolded, lined against a wall with guns aiming at your heads, be sure and tell them where to find me," he bellowed with mirth.

The Cajun shouted back. "You should worry about yourself. You're the one tied up," he gnarled. He cut his hard eyes back to me, "Rub dirt on your face and clothes. We need to get going."

I grabbed his arm before he stalked off. "Wait! What about the guys? We can't leave them unprotected."

"Don't worry," the Cajun nodded at Titan. "He's going to stay. Your friends are safe." He turned away climbing in the driver's seat.

I felt a sudden heavy hand on my shoulder. Startled, my gaze flew up at the person with the hand. "Don't worry Ms. Stevie," Titan smiled, missing a front tooth. "I'll take real good care of your friends." Titan nodded to Aidan, "That son of a bitch over there won't move an inch unless he wants a belly full of lead," he swore. "I got this!"

I smiled at the gentle giant and rubbed his arm. Then my attention focused back to Aidan. "Hold on!" I called out to the Cajun as he juiced the car's engine. I trotted over to Aidan. Just for peace of mind, I wanted to check the rope. I sat on my heels and tugged on the golden fire that encircled his body. I whispered a few words, solidifying the bind.

Once upon a time, I would've never worried about Aidan harming the guys. This *Aidan* was as trustworthy as a cottonmouth. There was a stir in my gut that gave me unease.

Titan might be tough as nails, capable of taking care of himself in any bar brawl. But he was no match against a perfidious druid. Dark magick had a way of gaining momentum even on the most fiercest.

If only I could be in two places at once. I bit my bottom lip, indecisive. What other choice did I have? I had to trust Titan and the magick rope. My gaze collided with Aidan. "If you hurt my friends, I will hunt you down to the far corners of this earth. You got that!" Ice rolled off my tongue.

Aidan's lips flat-lined and his eyes displayed blatant contempt. I stood up, hesitating, then with an abrupt sneer, I spun on my heels, kicking up dirt in his face.

Before I had a chance to climb in the Jeep, the Cajun leaned over to the passenger's side, cutting a firm gaze at me. "I'm in charge. You follow my orders and we live. *Comprende?*" Veins in his neck stood out in livid ridges.

I scoffed at his arrogance. I reckoned he didn't think a woman could handle herself. Or maybe, he felt he was the better man for the position because he'd fought in the Middle East. "Okay, Commander!" I saluted, snappy. "Whatever you say."

"*Bien!* I'll drive first," he barked. "I know how to navigate around all the potholes on the backroad. When we get out on the paved highway, you take the wheel. I'll take watch and handle the bombs."

The reality of the peril we were about to encroach upon was starting to sink in. I took a deep nervous breath and exhaled. "Okay, let's get rolling." I climbed in the passenger's seat and buckled up, clenching the grab bar and grinding my teeth.

~

Once we neared the outskirts of the city, I took over the wheel.

As we slowly rolled into downtown, I cut the lights so that we might slip past anyone looking for trouble.

The streets were nearly empty, only a handful of folks walking down the sidewalk. It was startling. All of them seemed in a trance, walking mindlessly, faces void of expression. It iced my bones. I thought of the patients at Haven Hospital. Walking and breathing but no light upstairs.

When we turned onto Bourbon Street, my heart squeezed. Only a block ahead, in plain sight, stood three regulators heavily armed. Their weapons were like nothing I'd ever seen. The foreign guns glistened with a weird metal, some sort of clear shield covering it. The barrel had to be the size of a small cannon. A sense of the willies rushed over me. We were screwed. Their advanced arms against our meager guns and homemade bombs were like bringing sparklers to a nuke war. The worst part I couldn't protect us. My unstable magick was useless against their technology. I eased out a prickly sigh.

These fat cats were not your typical police. A staggering seven foot or better in height and massive bodies, these regulators gave advanced science a whole new freak-on. They were clothed in gray uniforms that shined like metal. I couldn't get a good look at their faces. They wore a tinted bubbled shield over their heads. It was weird, the shield shifted, moving to the form of their head. Like nothing I'd ever seen. If I were a betting gal, I'd wager that our atmosphere was incompatible to their environment. If my hunch were right, having that little juice in my back pocket could give us an edge. Smash their helmets and watch 'em suffocate. Cruel, but effective.

Suddenly, my eyes locked onto three silver spheres, hovering a few feet above the regulators. An unnatural humming resonated from the silver balls. They zipped back and forth, turning and twisting. I think they were communicating. I first thought they were drones. Though, the spheres didn't resemble a drone at all or what I imagined, comparing them to Hollywood's version. Apart from popular belief, this was different, a new technology, my guess. The strange spheres were like liquid metal that glinted similar to a mirror, yet they moved like liquid, changing its form from a ball to a flat wafer of paper. Sci-fi movie of the fourth kind, I called it. Not taking my eyes off the strange metal, I whispered. "Nick, look up," I nodded curtly. "In your entire military career, have you ever seen a drone like that?"

The Cajun's eyes followed my fixation. "Damn!" he gasped. "*Non!* Drones do not look like that." He blew a low whistle.

I think for once, the Cajun and I were on the same page. We both knew we had underestimated the hostiles. This uprising placed eerie on a whole new platform.

We didn't utter another word, keeping our eyes glued. Any second this could go bad. I think the Cajun sensed it too by the clench in his jaw.

My eyes caught his, silently cuing for further instructions. The Cajun nodded, urging me to keep driving forward. Adrenaline coursed through my veins as I slowly crept along. My palms were sweaty, gripping the wheel as we slowly rolled past one of the regulators standing guard at the corner. We acknowledged his presence with a curt nod, hoping not to stir suspicion. Sweat beaded across my forehead and began to drip into my left eye. My first reaction was to wipe it off, but I withdrew. Instead, I kept my hands on the wheel with one clear eye.

Despite our caution, I had a whirl of doubts that we had managed to stay under the guards' radar. Blending was the plan, yet I think we made a huge mistake. We were the only ones with a vehicle and our eyes still had life. The locals I saw were on foot. As if marching to the same tune, they all parroted the same slow step and expression.

One of the regulators yelled out to us, "Halt, humans!" Fear stifled my breath. Without so much as a flick, I slipped a sideways glance at the Cajun. He remained poker faced.

I tapped the brake and rolled to an easy stop. My hands were white knuckling the wheel as my heart protested. I sat quiet, not uttering a word, keeping my face emotionless. Sweat poured from under my cap and it itched like a mother. Even still, I didn't make any sudden move. I waited for my cue, anticipating the worst scenarios possible.

The regulator loomed over the Jeep, investigating the contents loaded in the back. Without warning, he drew to attention, speaking sharply. "State your destination." His gruff voice hummed, like he was breathing through a trach tube. I slipped a sideways glance but all I could see was my reflection off the shield of his helmet.

The Cajun spoke, no detection of alarm in his deep voice. "We want to trade goods for food. You like crabs, yes?" the Cajun flashed his pearly whites, keeping his hands raised, as he slowly eased out of the Jeep, making his way to the back. He lifted one of the crate's lid revealing a large catch of snappers. The sound of splashing in the water and claws clicking wafted in the air.

The regulator peered into the crate, and then suddenly leaped backward, shrieking like a banshee. I reckoned it was the alien universal sound of fright. He mumbled something in his native tongue, quickly wagging his weapon at the Cajun, shouting, "Keep that closed! Pass earth-dweller and don't return," he muttered something in his own tongue. Strange enough, his language sounded similar to clicking his tongue over a loud mic. The Cajun jumped back in the Jeep as he slipped me a quick wink. His glint beamed with pride. I'd have to hand it to him, that was a smart move.

Getting past the regulator made us both breathe a little easier. Although, we came to a quick conclusion that we were not out of the alien corral just yet.

Around the corner in the French Quarter, I blinked, doubting my own eyes. The street was completely barren. No lights, no music, not a soul stirring. The once thriving street laid in total darkness. I couldn't believe my own eyes as I combed over the dark buildings. I was just here at *The Royal Café* eating dinner with Dom and Jeffery a few weeks ago. Now, it was gone. All of it was gone! The street was deserted like a long-forgotten ghost town.

Trash and broken glass splayed the street. Most of the buildings had broken windows. I stared blankly as the wind tossed an empty can across the street as it echoed in my ears. Other than our Jeep's engine, the can was the only noise.

I inclined my head slightly, speaking low where only Nick could hear. "I can't believe this is happening." My eyes darted wildly back and forth from one side of the street to the next.

The Cajun touched my shoulder and whispered pointedly. "Hush!"

I nodded, drawing my words to myself. Freaking out while we were in the middle of hell zone wasn't an option. I inhaled a ragged breath and I nearly gagged. The stench in the night's sultry air smelled of decayed, dead bodies. I held my hand to my nose. This took me back to the time when Sam nearly raped me in a field of bones and decay. All those bodies of women that Sam had viciously murdered. I was lucky then, Aidan swooping in and rescuing me from his psycho cousin. I inhaled a despairing sigh. How I wished that Aidan were here now. I shook the memory from my brain. I couldn't afford memory lane right now.

Especially now.

The Cajun tapped my thigh. I glanced down at a red bandana. I took it and parroted him, tying it around my neck and slipping the cloth over my nose and mouth. I nodded to him with a silent thank you.

As we ventured farther down, we spotted more zombie like people, creeping along, dragging their feet, clothes soiled and torn. Sadly, I knew that expressionless face far too well. They were homeless. I rolled past them, watching one by one, as they made their way down the street, heading in the same direction.

I spied several folks ahead, falling in line, farther down the street. I reckoned they had come for food rations. The Cajun and I shared a quick glimpse at each other. If his face mirrored mine, we were both sharing the same horror.

At the front of the line, a regulator hovered over an elderly woman. The creature was holding a small metal device over the woman's wrist. I had my suspicions that he was looking for the number Aidan boldly bragged about the other day, the digits, six six six. A sneaky feeling crept down my spine that it was more than just a mark. They were tagging people. Inserting implants to keep track of every soul or worse, using the tags to control. A sudden sharp twist to the gut made me flinch and I turned to the Cajun, "Nick," I whispered. "Whatever you do don't let them ink you. I think it's affecting the people." I glanced over at him, my eyes brimmed with worry.

Keeping his eyes steady ahead, he barely whispered, "I was thinking the same thing," he exhaled softly. "I think we've seen enough."

Nodding in compliance, I took a sharp turn down Pirate's Alley. The alley was a 600 foot long cobblestone, pedestrian street that ran between St. Louis Cathedral and Cabildo and was one of the most fabled streets in New Orleans, full of wild stories of the infamous, Jean Lafitte. As time passed, the alley seemed more suitable for tourists on foot. Jeffery and I used to grab lunch at the little café, named after the street, *Pirate's Alley Café*.

When I coiled the corner, alarm surged through me. I let up off the gas, gaping in silence. "Nick," I barely mumbled. The Cajun drew in a sharp gasp, though not uttering a word. His eyes held to what laid ahead.

As if it had never existed, the alleyway was in complete ruin, burned to the ground, left only with the stench of feces floating in the night's air and a charred heap scarfing the cobblestone. "They're destroying our city."

"*Oui!* This sickens me too," the Cajun grated, "Let's get out of this hell."

Before Nick and I could pull ourselves together, three regulators stepped out from behind the corner building at the end of the alleyway into plain sight, guns aiming and blocking the exit.

My foot hit the brake, "Nick! We got company."

"Back up, slowly," he spoke low as tension fostered his face. I slowly shifted the gears into reverse and pressed the gas, backing up. Two more regulators stepped from the shadows, barricading us in at both entrances. I knew we were in deep crap up to our necks, maybe more. Hell, we didn't even have an escape plan. Luckily, my daggers laid safely tucked underneath my clothes, sheathed and ready to go into action. Their light hum soothed me.

All at once, Nick snatched a jug of

moonshine from the back and hung half his body over the grab-bar of the Jeep, taking a sloppy swig. When he came back up for air, he wiped his mouth with the back of his hand and waved the gallon in the air at the regulators. His words slurred as if he'd polished off the whole jug. "*Hey,* you *b-b-boys* want some *gud* old corn w-whiskey, *yessss?* It will w-wet your whistle and make the ladies spread their legs!" He staggered, taking another big gulp. It was clear to me now that the Cajun was sidetracking their attention from us to the whiskey.

The regulators paused as confusion eddied their stride. Heads snapping amidst each other, and then back at Nick and me.

Our engagement must've startled them. That was a no brainer. I doubted any local was capable of a simple "*hello*".

I watched, not making a move as they slowly etched forward. Mistrust dabbled the humid air as they approached us, keeping their weapons drawn, pointing straight at our heads. Slowly they etched closer. It seemed his boozehound manner eased the regulators, making them more curious than trigger-happy.

Trapped in the alleyway, Nick and I sat

helpless like chickens caught in a hen house with a fox.

Alarm bristled my spine as I hissed under my breath. "Whatever you're doing, it better work!"

The Cajun ignored me as if he'd forgotten that I was sitting in the driver's seat. I stiffened, waiting for the next move either by the Cajun or the regulators. At this point, I wasn't sure which was worse.

Nerves squeezed my gut as I sat there silent, hands clenching the steering wheel, white knuckled and sweaty palms.

I flinched slightly as the regulators corralled the Jeep, banging their weapons against the rear. A downwind draft shimmied up my nose, nearly causing me to lose my cookies. I held my breath to avoid vomiting. I didn't know if it was an alien thing, but their smell reminded me of rotten eggs.

The Cajun was playing the juicehead far too well. I prayed that his acting skills worked. "You soldiers like some of the best homemade moonshine in *New Or-lins?* Gotta jug with your name on it." The Cajun patted the large glass jar as he sloppily leaned over dragging out a couple of bottles and offering them to the regulators.

At first, the creatures hesitated. To my surprise, one regulator snatched one of the jugs from Nick with lightning speed. I stayed quiet while I watched from the corner of my eye, avoiding eye contact. The regulator held the glass jug up looking at the white liquid. He spoke to the others in that strange tongue-clicking dialect.

The large regulator kept shaking his head trying to knock the jug out of his comrade's hand. Finally, the smaller creature holding the jug shoved the larger one back and appeared to be possessive of his new discovery as he raised his voice at the other four. The shorter one lowered his shield, opening his large mouth, tipping the jug to his mouth.

I nearly choked on my breath trying to stifle a gasp. His features were human like, but his skin was scaly, and his eyes were almond shape and cold black.

The short regulator immediately started gasping. He pulled it together and cut his black eyes at Nick. A smiled stretched his scaly face, revealing sharp jagged teeth. He tilted the jug and took another gulp. Nick nodded with approval urging the creature to drink up. "*Gud!* Yes?" he encouraged, smiling.

In the next second, the larger regulator

grabbed the other jug from the short one and lowered his shield revealing a very similar face. The bigger one tipped the jug to his cracked lips and wrapped his brown scaly lips around the mouth of the bottle, downing the moonshine.

At that point, they all seemed to share deep interest in our drink. After the ticking of a few moments, the five regulators had lowered their shields, passing the moonshine around. Strangely, their behavior reminded me of humans.

I understood now what the Cajun was doing. He was diverting their attention and it was working. The moonshine was taking effect on the creatures and fast too. Even in their own hideous language, their words were slurring. One of the regulators aggressively leaned into the Jeep shouting at Nick, "Give us more of this strange liquid!" He demanded as he commenced shoving the crates around and nearly knocking over a few.

Nick jumped in the back before our cover was blown, grabbing up more jugs, "Here!" He held two jugs in each hand. "Compliments, please!" It seemed to appease the creatures' burst of anger and appealed to their greedy thirsts. It wasn't long before they'd forgotten about us. They huddled together, guzzling down the corn liquor, laughing and patting each other on the back.

Without delay, the Cajun motioned for me to punch the gas. I gladly put the Jeep in gear and accelerated, burning rubber down the alleyway.

The regulators didn't even bother looking up. I took a sharp turn down Anne Street and hooked it onto Decatur.

But we weren't out of the woods yet. I spotted a regulator heading our way, chasing, and shouting something incomprehensible. I wasn't sticking around to find out what he wanted. I gunned the Jeep picking up speed. Besides, there was nothing I hated worse than a seven-foot alien throwing a temper tantrum in my rearview mirror.

The creature was gaining on us at an inhuman speed. The Cajun shouted, "Floor this damn Jeep!"

I peered in the mirror to see if we were gaining momentum. Unfortunately, our Jeep had nothing on this creature. Just when he grasped the back of the Jeep, the creature hoisted himself up on the cab. With no time to spare, the Cajun slammed a balloon into the creature's face.

The homemade bomb exploded knocking the Cajun off his feet and tumbling on top of me. Lucky for us, the regulator had taken off his shield and the fluid spattered across his face and into his eyes. He screeched like something out of a horror movie. For the Cajun and me, it confirmed our hopes that the bomb would work. The creature fell backwards hitting the hard pavement, face first. The Cajun and I bellowed with triumph, high fiving each other.

STEAL AWAY

Once we got back to the Cajun's house, I wanted to kiss the ground. After I cut the engine, the Cajun jumped out of the Jeep. I slid out of the driver's seat and ran after him. "Wait!" I called to him. "Are you okay?" Not one word uttered between us the whole trip back. I didn't know about the Cajun, but my body was trembling.

The Cajun stopped in his tracks and turned abruptly to face me. A wide smile plagued his face. "*Oui!* That got my motor revved."

"You're kidding? Do you have any concept of what just happened?"

"I do! Aliens are running amok." His dark eyes glistened.

"I think it's a bit more than creatures running haywire. Our world is under siege by freaking aliens!"

The Cajun raked his fingers through his sable waves. "One thing you must know about me," he pointed to his chest, "I know war better than most. I even received a medal of honor. But it meant nothing." His face grew pinched with anger.

"Have you ever fought against creatures such as these?" I stepped up closer, meeting him toe to toe, forcing him to look at me. I had to make him understand what we were up against.

The Cajun's jaw twitched. "War is war, *babé*! I've seen my men who trusted me with their lives get blown to pieces and none of those highfalutin officials cared. My men died for a senseless war. A war that wasn't ours to fight. You say Freedom Fighters. I say there is no freedom in fighting. Those young men didn't have a say. So, in my opinion, it doesn't matter who we fight. We do the best we can with what we have and pray there's a God to deliver us from the Devil himself."

I stood there lost for words. How could I argue? He was right. We didn't fight for *our* freedom. Innocent people gave their lives for leaders that were setup to fail while all along the Illuminati had full sovereignty. Those in the forefront were merely puppets on a string. I inhaled a sharp breath as I replied, "I'm sorry." I jerked my cap off and wiped the sweat from my face with the back of my hand. "You're right." We both stood there in an awkward silence, our eyes glued to each other.

Then my heart lurched. I skimmed the grounds. A strange sensation rushed through me. Everything was too quiet, not even the stir of birds chirping, the cicadas cricking, and the house inside, not one light, just darkness. Something was wrong. The Cajun kept the generator running. And Jeffery didn't like the dark. Even Titan hadn't shown his face. I thought someone would've came out to greet us by now. But there wasn't a peep.

An eerie breeze blew through my damp hair as my blood iced.

"Oh my God, Dom and Jeffery!" My alarm soared to the moon as I sprinted for the house. I called for my knives as they followed my commands, unsheathe, resting on my shoulder, waiting for word to attack. I stepped into the darkness as the Cajun followed closely behind me with his gun in hand and cocked, ready to fire. We padded quietly without a sound throughout the house. No signs of anyone! But all of Dom's and Jeffery's clothes were still here. My pulse raced in my throat as my worse fear began to sink into my skull.

The Cajun called out to me as he switched a light on. "Come here!" he shouted. I followed his stressful voice. The Cajun was standing in the kitchen by the table holding a note. Quickly, I snatched it from his hand and read it out loud.

Sorry to leave before saying my good-byes. I'm taking the boys with me. If you want your little gay friends, you know where to find them. Don't wait too long. They may end up like your friend.

When we meet again,
Aidan

Before I took my next breath, the Cajun had charged out the door, heading straight for the storage. I raced after him as my gut roiled every step of the way. I sensed this wasn't good. I could smell Titan's fate wafting in the air.

When the Cajun threw open the doors, the stench struck our nostrils, jolting us back. I gagged, covering my mouth. The unusual heat had sped up the decay making the fetor more than insufferable. Holding back vomit, I tugged my bandana over my mouth and nose.

The Cajun slowly entered the storage, dropping to his knees, his face stricken with grief.

I gasped realizing the ferocity of what length Aidan would go to was terrifying.

Titan's body hung on two heavy oak limbs, tied with my rope into a cross, nails driven into his hands, legs, and one large stake pierced through his head.

As if frozen in time, Titan's face was the poster of horror. His mouth stretched wide into an O as if he'd been screaming at the top of his lungs. I had a strong suspicion that Titan's death was a slow torturous one. His missing eyeballs were now an empty cavity brimmed with blood. As if he'd been dipped into a bucket of scarlet red paint, his whole face and beard were saturated. Shear black fear pummeled through my skull as my eyes raked over Titan's body. Guts dangled from the gaping hole in his stomach and by the deep indentions that wrapped around his neck, my guess was that Aidan had slit his throat.

I spied bloody handprints over the cross and Titan's body. I suspected the handprints belonged to Aidan. Footprints, large and smaller ones collected around Titan's body. It was clear to me that two people were involved. One being a *woman*.

If I were a betting gal, I'd bet it was Sally. Who else would come to rescue Aidan and assist in a gruesome murder? *His uncle, Van?* Possibly, but I doubted it. Van would've sent for one of his MIB, *men in black*.

I had to admit that this murder didn't seem like the work of Aidan. It was too messy for a 300-year-old druid. To put it candidly, Aidan didn't do sloppy. Everything about Aidan was precise, right down to the last detail. Keeping that little tidbit in mind had me muddled. The details about this murder screamed volumes to look deeper.

The untidy letter came to mind. Whoever wrote the letter had unsteady hands. Like someone nervous. Aidan didn't do shaky.

Nothing made sense. My brain told me Aidan murdered Titan, yet there weren't any telltale signs that this was his doing.

For example, I noticed the trail of blood

through the yard, up the steps, leading to inside the storage room. Obviously, they had dragged Titan's body. That seemed odd to me.

They called him Titan for a reason. The man outstood most with a height nearly seven feet and his belt size most likely had to be special ordered.

Why would a druid do such a human task? Aidan could've killed Titan with the flick of his hand and conjured up a cross with Titan's body nailed to it, not getting even a drop of blood on himself or anything else. He certainly wouldn't need assistance. It was clear Titan's death had a meaning, definitely a sadistic one, but this wasn't the work of a druid. It was more like a human with tons of strength.

I saw how easily Aidan had taken down a fey, Sam, and disposed of his body in a matter of minutes. I inhaled a ragged breath. My eyes combed over the murder scene as I shook my head, puzzled. I didn't see the consistency in the two murders.

I glanced over to the Cajun. He was taking his friend's death hard. Understandably. Tears swelled. This was my fault. If I'd just gone off on my own, Titan would be alive, and the guys would be safe too. Aidan only took Dom and Jeffery because he knew how important they were to me. What a fool I'd been, thinking that my rope would've kept him captive. Aidan had tricked me and now I had cost human lives.

My stomach started to erupt as I darted for the deck, stopping in the nick of time, puking up my guts. I'd seen gruesome things in my life before, but this was incomparable.

After I finished, I wiped my mouth with my sleeve and collapsed on the steps. I buried my head into my palms as my body shook, racked with sobs. I reckoned that was the human in me.

I heard the Cajun murmuring curse words and feeble prayers in French as he pulled out the nails from Titan's body. My heart ached for him and I wanted to console him. Despite my good intentions, I knew he blamed me for this tragedy. I was sure that my face was the last thing he wanted to see.

"God!" I shivered trying to make sense of this monstrosity. That poor man was tortured to death. This murder or more appropriately, butchering, was a message. Aidan had left that especially for me. He meant to frighten me, and it worked. Any humanity that Aidan once possessed had been totally depleted, leaving him nothing short of a monster. He had taken my family. I feared the worst. I had to pull myself together and get Jeffery and Dom back before Aidan hurts them like he did Titan. I hoped as long as they remained a bargaining tool, Aidan would keep them alive. "Geez!" I raked my fingernails over my face. How would we all survive this devastation? I hadn't a clue what I should do next. How was I supposed to find them? I might have angel blood, but I didn't have a GPS. I didn't even have wings.

Heavy footsteps startled me. I stiffened as my eyes froze on the Cajun's face, his eyes blazing murderously. With no warning, he grabbed me by my collar and jerked me to my feet. His deep inky eyes glistened with raw odium as he snarled in my face, "I thought you said that *couillon* (scoundrel) was tied down. Obviously, your magic rope didn't work. Or did you loosen it so he could get away?" The Cajun dropped his grip, shoving me backward, twisting my feet into a near stumble, but I caught the railing.

I shot back. "I did check the rope! Do you think I wanted this too?" My tears swallowed up my last word.

A swift shadow of rage swept across the Cajun's face. "*Non!* Stop crying!" he leaned closer. "You didn't do a good enough job! My *ami* is *dead* and most likely your boys are too!"

I shoved the Cajun out of my personal space, "I know better than anyone what Aidan's capable of *doing*! I'm-I'm sorry for your friend." Tears rolled down my cheeks as I wiped them with my sleeve.

"What kind of fucking creature is your ex-lover?"

"Stop calling him my ex!" I shouted. My shame quickly turned into stabbing anger.

"There's something unearthly about that boy. That upside-down cross is suspended in air! Floating! No wires dangling it. Can you explain that to me?"

"What?" I was caught off guard. "What are you talking about?"

The Cajun grabbed my arm, dragging me along with his deep stride. "Come see for yourself!" he bit out through gritting teeth.

Standing in the doorframe, the Cajun dropped his grip abruptly. I glared at him as if he'd lost his damn mind. "Tell me what you see."

I studied the cross up to the rope that tied the cross to the beam. I turned to the Cajun. "The cross isn't floating." I pointed to one of the high beam. "Don't you see the yellow rope?" I stared back at him.

The Cajun sputtered, bristling with indignation. "Are referring to *your* rope?"

My brows dipped into a scowl. "No! I mean the rope hanging from the beam."

He stared, complete disgust on his face. "*Non!* I see only your magical rope. *Vous devez être aveugle!* (You must be blind!)"

"Me blind!" I shouted. "You're the blind one here!"

By the lines of his tight face, I could see that we both were on the brink of insanity.

"I don't see a rope!" he grated.

Then as it hit me, my eyes orbed like golf balls. "I think I know what's happening here."

"Spit it out!"

I looked up at the rope and then my eyes locked onto the Cajun's face. "It's not real, Nick! What you are seeing is an illusion. The kind of illusions fey create."

"I am not imagining things!"

"What you are seeing is something like a mirage."

"Are you saying Titan is not dead?"

"No, no! I'm sorry, but Titan is gone. I think Sally came to help Aidan escape. She has to be fey." My eyes kept shifting back and forth to Titan's body and then to the Cajun. "It makes sense."

"Maybe to you but not to me." The Cajun threw his hands to his hips, shooting bullets at me.

"Listen to me!" I demanded, wishing I could slap some sense into him. "Your grandmother had the gift and you know that Val and I are angels."

The Cajun didn't deign to answer.

"Look, I know how crazy it sounds but think about it. You know humans are not the only creatures. The night before Aidan and Sally took me away, Sam had tricked me into believing that he was Aidan. Sam had taken me to a field of lilies. Only it was an illusion. Fey cannot conjure up tangible items. Underneath the glamor, I was standing in a field of bones and decay." I pointed to the yellow rope. "What you are seeing is a Fey's glamor, an *illusion*." I gave pause. "I think Aidan's partner, Sally, is fey."

"Huh! Like little fairies with wings, yes?" The Cajun made a mocking gesture with his fingers.

"Nick, that's fairytale stuff. Fey are vile and evil. They are notorious for their skullduggery." I suddenly felt my stomach roil once again. In a snap, I spun on my heels and headed out to the deck. I needed fresh air.

I stopped at the steps and bent over, hands on my knees to brace myself for my next purge. Guilt, loathing, and sorrow weighed heavily on my chest. I hated myself right now.

The Cajun startled me when he came up from behind. "Are you, alright?" His gentle voice pierced my thoughts.

I squared my shoulders, standing up, wiping my mouth with the back of my hand as our eyes locked. "No, I don't think either one of us are going to be okay. Not after today."

"It sure is looking that way, yes?" The Cajun quiet for a moment. "What is this creature you once loved?"

"Aidan's immortal and he draws dark magick from his druid heritage," I said. "He's invincible."

"I remember you calling him druid." The Cajun exhaled a raspy breath, "I thought that was a nickname. And he can't die!" the Cajun half yelled at me. "How could you have forgotten to mention this little piece of information to me?" The insolence in his voice was sharp as a razor.

"Honestly, I don't know why!" I swallowed hard. My throat ached from sheer guilt. "I thought I had Aidan contained."

"What else are you not telling me?" Nick's

face darkened like a thunderstorm. "Don't hold back!"

I couldn't look him in the eyes. His dark eyes glistened with pain and enmity. I held my gaze to the tree line. "I think Aidan's trying to draw me out from hiding. That much I am certain of. Why else would he have taken Dom and Jeffery?"

The Cajun stood there gawking at me with the look of wanting to throttle me. Under the heat of his blaze, I felt like crawling under a rock. But I knew that checking out wouldn't make any of this go away. I had to be accountable for my mistakes even if it meant my death.

The Cajun spoke through clenched teeth. "I have to bury my friend. Then we need to get the hell out of here. It's not safe." He stalled for a moment as if he wanted to say something else. Then without another word, he stormed off.

I watched as he disappeared behind the back of the house. I whirled on my heels, not sure what I should do next. I needed to help, to be useful.

Nick had a right to be angry with me. I had cost him his best friend's life and possibly Dom and Jeffery's too. I should've stayed behind to guard Aidan myself. Titan should've gone with Nick. Why didn't I listen to Jeff?

I struggled, fighting off a meltdown. Tears were pushing to the forefront. Instead of letting go, I bit against the burn.

My eyes stalled on the chopped up oak that once held Aidan captive. I stared at it as a gentle breeze rustled through my hair. Curiosity jump kicked me into action as I stalked down the steps and over to the once thriving tree.

As my eyes skimmed the ground, I spotted tracks... *Aidan's*. Somehow, he'd managed to cut himself free of my magickal rope but not without injury. Scarlet red churned in the dirt. Lots of it too.

I spotted a procession of footprints mixed with a lot of blood. Three different sizes circled the tree. The soil and bloodshed disturbed the ground as if Freddie Krueger had driven a John Deer tractor through a crowd of bystanders. Apparently, there was a struggle. It looked like Titan had given Aidan a good fight.

The night was embarking, and a strange chill hung in the air as I shivered. I spotted the security light. It was out. From what I could tell, someone had thrown a rock, busting the bulb. Tiny pieces of glass pooled around the pole and a large rock laid only a couple of feet away. I scratched my head, baffled. Taking in account of a bloody brawl and a light bulb busted, which none of this made any sense. Why would Aidan get into a physical altercation with a human? Come to think about it... since Aidan's return, I hadn't seen him do one magick act. More missing pieces to add to the puzzle.

I turned around and found more footsteps leading to the house. I could quickly pick out the sizes and the kind of tread on the bottom. Aidan's footprints were easy. Jeffery's and Dom's too. I squatted to get a closer look. By the shuffle in the dirt, it appeared that the guys were forced against their will. It was as though they had been dragged out of the house. Fear dug into my chest.

Suddenly my eyes landed on tire tracks. These set of tracts belonged to an unknown car. On the left side of the tracks, I spotted a female's footprints. Small though wide, like a chubby person. The same bloody footprints in the shed. My suspicions were confirmed that Sally was somewhere in the mix of this crime.

I noticed the flurry of footprints stopped, ending on the right side of the tire tracks. It appeared the wheels sped out, kicking up a huge cloud of dirt. Obviously, they were in a rush.

I found that strange. If Aidan were in a hurry, why would he wait for transportation when he could've materialized to any location in seconds?

I inhaled a sharp breath, biting my bottom lip. It didn't matter that Sally or Tom Dick and Harry had helped Aidan escape. The height of my worry was that Aidan was free and unpredictably dangerous and all the more reason why I had to find him before he killed Dom and Jeffery.

THE LION'S DEN

I stood quietly as the Cajun threw on the last shovel of dirt. He marked the grave with a couple of plyboards nailed together. He carved into the wood Titan's legal name,

John Mack, CPL US Marine Corps,
Afghanistan War 2012-2015
Born: July 15, 1986, Died: July 9, 2020

It was short and to the point. The Cajun whispered a few words to his dear friend. I stood back a few feet, quiet, feeling like an intruder. I gulped down the knot lodged in my throat. I didn't have a right to cry. So, I swallowed the pain and didn't dare utter a word.

Once Nick finished giving his respect, our eyes locked for the first time since he'd left me to go bury Titan. "We need to get going. The boat's loaded with supplies." His words were cold, and all emotions depleted. I knew better though. Inside, the man was broken over the loss of his friend. I admired his strength and hated his condemning eyes that singed my heart. Though the blame was all mine. I'd carry that blame for the rest of my life, too.

"The boat?" I was taken aback.

"You have a problem riding in a boat?" He brushed the remaining dirt from his hands as a faint line appeared between his brows.

"We have to go looking for Jeffery and Dom!"

"Are you *crazy*?" the Cajun growled. "Those boys are dead!"

"Don't say that!"

"We go back to town and we are as good as dead, gul!"

I stood my ground, determined. "Fine! I'll go without you."

The Cajun stood silent for a moment, staring a hole through me. Then he said with a huff, "You don't even know where to look."

"There's a good chance that Aidan's holding the guys hostage at his mansion on the outskirts of town. We can take the backroads. It should be safe enough."

The Cajun's face took on the look of an angry bear. "Past the sugar cane fields?"

"Yes."

"Are you that naïve or just stupid?" his voice grated harshly. "You're walking into a trap."

"I still have to go!"

The Cajun stepped up even closer, looming over me. "Do you think he's going to hand over your love ones?" his lips tightened as his hands flexed into a tight ball. "That *le diable* (devil) is too fucking evil."

My eyes tensed, no flinching as I held my stance. "He might not have a choice if I kill him."

"You think you can kill that bastard?" Doubt laced his voice. "*Non!* You won't." he flashed a seedy grin.

"Where's your faith in me, Nick?" Any kindred feelings for Aidan had been long gone. I blamed him for the loss of my child. And now, he'd taken the only two people in the world that meant anything to me. "You've underestimated me." I spoke in a mere whisper but there was nothing calm about my words or my intentions.

"You might have angel magick," he said as he fingered his two-day-old stubble, "but it's not going to do much good, gul. *You* still love him." The Cajun's words stabbed me viciously.

"Listen, Cajun!" I jabbed my finger into his chest. "The Aidan I once loved is not in that animal that killed your friend and kidnapped my family. The Aidan I once loved is dead!" I clenched my teeth. "Dead! *Il est mort* (he is dead)! Got that?"

"I heard you the first time!"

"Good! Don't get it confused." I stormed off jumping in the Jeep. I tossed over my shoulder, not looking at his face. "You coming or staying? Either way, I'm going after that son of a bitch!"

He hesitated kicking at the dirt. "Fine!" he grinded out. "Give me a minute. I need to radio the others and warn them." He swiftly spun on his heels darting into the house. I laid my head on the steering wheel and let out a scream of frustration. How the hell did I get myself into this mess? The world was crumbling around me. My family was gone, taken as hostages. I'd give anything to go back in time to a much simpler life. I wished I were eight again and my dad was alive. I wished Sara hadn't fallen prey to greed and I'd been born an average child. Rather than a freak created in a lab by the Illuminati's scientist. Boy, I didn't want much.

The Cajun insisted on driving. I didn't have it in me to argue. So, I gladly gave him the wheel as I slid to the passenger seat. We were off down the dirt road and on the major highway before the Cajun struck up a conversation. The Cajun cleared his throat. "I apologize for accusing you of ..."

I butted in, stopping him in midstream, "Nick! *Don't*! I should've stayed behind. Titan's death is my fault. I was wrong not warning you or Titan about Aidan's magick." I let out a painful sigh. "You were right." Our eyes met briefly, and I saw pity in the Cajun's eyes. I hated it too.

For the remainder of the ride, we didn't talk. Although, I felt torn about the Cajun coming, even still, I was glad. He may be human, though he proved his usefulness. I only hoped I didn't get him killed. Too much bloodshed had been spilt already.

When we got on the edge of the city, the Cajun drew me from my thoughts. "Where is the bastard's mansion?"

My face twisted, lips squeezed, full of apprehension. I knew he wasn't going to like what I had to say next. The truth was sort of tucked away in my pocket. "Hmm, I wasn't entirely honest with you." I said feeling unease. "Aidan's not holding the men at his mansion. It's actually on Bourbon Street at Val's bar."

"You got to be fucking kidding me!" he clenched his jaw.

I shrugged.

"You purposely lied to me!" A slew of French curses paraded from his mouth.

I eased a sharp sigh. "I did. I had to!"

"*Non!* I'm not dying for you!" Swiftly, he cut the steering wheel to the left, heading back.

With no time to waste, I went into action. My angel powers kicked into gear. Before he knew what had happened, I'd thrown him to the back of the Jeep as I swiftly slid into the driver's seat. With my foot on the break, I twisted in my seat, staring back at him as he lay wedged between two crates. "Look!" My voice rose. "You promised Val you'd protect me! Are you a man of your word or not?" I was wearing determination like an armored suit. The Cajun was going with me whether he liked it or not. In my book, a promise was a promise.

The look of shock veiled his face for a minute. Grumbling to himself, with more French curse words, he managed to wiggle himself free from the two crates. Sitting up, he sneered. "True. I promised Valor. *But* I didn't sign up for this!" The exasperation in his voice came out like a swift, left hook. "While serving my country, I saw enough death that I wish I could erase from my mind. Every time I close my eyes, those images haunt me." He glimpsed away, pain colored his face as if he were reliving the atrocities. His gaze returned back to me. "Good soldiers blown to pieces with their intestines hanging out. Or their bodies ripped in two, lying in their own pool of blood." He raked his fingers roughly through his brown hair. "But this has me breaking out in a cold sweat. Not because I fear death. I've kissed the face of death more times than I care to count. What I fear is those poor people. They're getting slaughtered for nothing. It's like the Holocaust all over again. Only this time, it's every human being regardless of race. And the worst part, we've lost the fucking battle before it's begun. Our world isn't ours any longer. The human race is an endangered species. How can we fight that?"

It was hard listening to him. I felt his pain and shared his pessimism. "Those are my concerns too," I pushed. "If we don't fight, they'll surely win. Isn't it better to at least give it our all?" My eyes pleaded with him.

His deep browns softened. "Those two boys mean a lot to you, yes?"

I held my breath for a second. That damn knot in my throat again. I swallowed. "I'd give my life for them." Tears collected, burning my eyes.

The Cajun half teased. *"Only your life?* I thought you loved these boys?" his lip tipped up, almost into a smile. Then a cold silence fell between us. He went on to say, "We're headed straight for the lion's den. Those little bastards better appreciate me risking my ass."

I smiled back, half laughing. "They will be but be easy on the skinny one. He's just full of piss and vinegar."

The Cajun laughed shaking his head. "Hell,

let's get this party started. I hate being late to a fight," he leaped into the passenger seat. I put the stick in gear and punched the pedal to the metal.

~

It was well after midnight when we slowly rolled onto Bourbon Street. Strangely, the stars weren't out and as far as I could tell, there wasn't any cloud coverage either. The sky was a vacuum of blackness. Farther down the street, there was a heavy cloud of fog. Right away, I sensed an eeriness that lodged in my throat. I didn't like the look of this one bit.

I cut the lights, hoping we'd go unnoticed. The street was vacant. Not even the locals were to be seen. The air felt nulled as if the atmosphere suffered from depletion of oxygen. Sulfur lingered in my mouth, along with the stifling humidity. Not the usual Louisiana sultry heat, but something else, something *unnatural.*

Once we reached Val's bar, I spotted the sign that once lit the sidewalk with its bright neon lights. Now only one bulb flickered. An annoying buzz skidded down my spine as the sign squeaked on its last hinge. Just like every other establishment downtown, Val's bar lacked the vibrant life it once formerly possessed. A sense of loss washed over me as I quietly inhaled a sharp breath.

Jarring me from my thoughts, the Cajun nudged me to park under the stairwell. I nodded in compliance. I eased the Jeep up on the curve and parked it under the stairwell. It was a tight fit, but I managed to pull it off. The shadows promised safety rather than parking the Jeep in the street. With the streetlights out, the Jeep camouflaged into the darkness.

With my magickal daggers following closely behind like faithful pets, I jumped from the driver's seat and started for the stairs. The Cajun swiftly grabbed my upper arm, halting me. One of my daggers swiftly dropped between the Cajun and me, hovering right in his face, ready to deliver a fatal blow to the head.

He raised his palms surrendering, slowly backing up. "I mean no harm. I simply want to take the lead," he explained, agitated. "Do you mind calling your dog off?" he whispered angrily, nodding to my dagger.

"Sorry! She's trained to attack upon any aggression."

"That's why you should keep your puppies in an ironclad lockbox."

At a flick of the wrist, my dagger returned to her previous position.

The Cajun cocked his pistol, quietly advancing up the stairwell. I followed just as light-footed. I nearly laughed at his little gun. Looking at our visitors' weaponry, I'd reckon around this neck of the woods, his choice of protection was useless. I hoped luck was on our side that he wouldn't have to use it.

Without making a sound, we halted at Val's apartment door. The Cajun leaned in, putting his ear to the door, listening for any signs of life. He raised his gun up to his shoulder. Our eyes locked as he nodded for us to proceed.

Obviously, he didn't detect anything alarming. He may have felt the close was clear, but if I were right about *this* Aidan, the silence meant trouble.

The Cajun gently jiggled the doorknob. The knob didn't budge. He glanced back at me and whispered in my ear, "Do you have any suggestions?"

I paused, biting my bottom lip. I had to get inside Val's pad. Aidan could've left a clue.

Funny, how things just came to me. It was like breathing. I didn't know how I knew but I just did. I quietly stepped past the Cajun and stood in front of the door. I placed my hand around the knob and whispered a few druid words, twisting my hand a certain angle, snapping my wrist. The door crept open. I smiled to myself. At least, something good came from my infusion with Aidan.

The Cajun blinked at me in disbelief. The starkness in his eyes painted a vivid picture. We stepped inside. The pad was empty. No sign of life. The Cajun grabbed a chair setting it under the doorknob. It might secure the door for a minute, long enough for us to draw our weapons. Even then, I had my doubts. Judging by the size of one of those creatures, it wouldn't take much of a shove to jar the door open.

The Cajun pulled out his flashlight, giving us a steady stream of light to scout out Val's place. As my eyes combed over the dusty apartment, a swirl of memories came to mind. A touch of sadness struck me as I flopped down on the couch. I felt jilted. Val left us here alone to fend for ourselves. His race meant more to him than the guys and my safety and the safety of these poor people who were defenseless. The sting of disappointment grated against me and all I wanted to do was lay my face into my hands and have a good cry. But big girls didn't cry. I pushed off the couch and said to the Cajun, "Nick, there's nothing here except dust and empty memories."

"Let's move on to his bar," I huffed. The Cajun ignored my suggestion and started dragging out Val's frozen food from the freezer.

"What are you doing?"

"Val left all this food, beef, ribs, TV dinners, pot pies. The food's still frozen. It's wasting here."

I stood there blinking, just staring, mouth gaping. Then I yielded. What did I care? Val had left and no hope of him ever returning. "Go ahead!" I waved my hand. "I reckon your right."

"I don't recall needing your permission," the Cajun flashed a seedy grin. "But thanks anyway." He grabbed a trash bag from under the sink and raked the frozen foods inside the bag, tying it up. He shouldered the bag as we exited the apartment. It tugged on me taking Val's food. I didn't know why it bothered me. I reckoned it hit home knowing that I'd never see Val again. I suddenly stopped. Thinking about a past that no longer existed was only punishing myself. I had to get my head in the game. So, I pushed my feelings down to the dark place where forgetful memories lie. I had enough to worry about than fretting over some stupid food and a man. Tomorrow would be a brand new day and a whole set of different problems. Life sure was grand, I laughed to myself bitterly.

After leaving Val's pad, we eased our way down to the bar. When we reached the entrance, we stopped abruptly. The Cajun and I shared a brusque glance as suspicion between us went red alert. Someone had been here, leaving the double doors open.

My breath hung in my throat as the Cajun calmly eased the door wider. The door creaked, taking me to some horror flick. With his gun cocked, the Cajun went first. I stayed on his heels with my trusty knives hovering close to my shoulders.

When we stepped inside, we were quickly doused with blackness. The Cajun flipped on his flashlight and carefully combed over the establishment. I shook my head, disgusted. "This has to be the handy work of the regulators. They ransacked the place!" The chairs were disheveled, and thrown about, along with the broken and dismantled tables that were not much more than splinters of wood.

"*Baise-moi!*" the Cajun cursed softly. "These regulators are grimy bastards."

"Let's check out the storage." I nudged the Cajun.

"You lead."

To our surprise, nothing had been disturbed. Liquor bottles were in order in the showcase behind the register. "*Nous sommes de la chance! De l'alcool!* (We are in luck. Alcohol!) the Cajun mumbled with glee. Wasting no time, he made a beeline for the shelved liquor, snatching the bottles down, stacking them in an empty crate.

I stood there glaring at him. "Have you lost your damn mind?" I held my stance with my hands resting on my hips. "This isn't a looting party!"

I ordered my knives to return back to their sheath. I felt safe enough to put my girls back. There was no immediate threat of any intruders in the bar.

The Cajun gathered a box in his arms and pointedly replied, "*Oui!* I remember well and I might as well make the best of this lousy search and rescue," he grinned heading for the Jeep.

I rolled my eyes, but I didn't try to stop

him. Let him have all the liquor in the world. He might be easier to deal with perhaps. I spotted a bottle of Jack Daniels and snatched it off the bar. I opened the fresh bottle as my mouth watered for the soothing gold liquid. Hell, a little liquor might lift our spirits a bit. I threw my head back and guzzled down a strong gulp. It burned all the way down as I coughed up air, but the numbness soon kicked in and all I could think about was drinking myself into a stupor. I needed a moment to check out just to reboot.

I found my way to the back. The walk-in cooler was still cold and soothing against the sultry heat that had been astronomical. I wanted to bathe in it. The coolness gave my skin chills, but it felt so good against my singeing skin. I pulled my cap off and wiped the sweat off my forehead. I blew out a relaxing sigh. "Whew! I'd forgotten how good air conditioning felt." I closed my eyes and took another swig of the liquor. I couldn't remember the last time I had a good night's sleep. Then I thought about Dom and Jeffery. A pain stabbed at my heart. I needed to think where Aidan could've taken the guys. My mind just drew a blank as I gulped down more whiskey.

When the Cajun returned, he found me

sitting on the floor leaning back against a shelf. He paused for a brief second, and then joined me on the floor. Not uttering a word, the Cajun reached over taking the bottle from my grip, turning it up to his lips, taking a long swig. "Too sweet!" He drew the bottle from his mouth, scowling, and passed it back to me.

"My mom liked Jack Daniels."

"Where is your *mère* (mother) now?"

"Dead," I stated as I took another drink and passed it back.

"How did she die?" the Cajun asked, taking the bottle.

"She was poisoned by angel dust."

"Angel dust?"

"Yeah, it's crushed up fey gems. It's very potent and deadly."

"How did your *mère* find such a rare concoction?"

"The dust belonged to Aidan." I never was one for beating around the bush.

No more than my admittance, the Cajun started coughing after he'd swallowed a huge gulp of liquor. I reckoned he wasn't ready for that shocker. "Your boyfriend poisoned your own *mère*?!" he choked out the words.

"I once thought it was my doing. I had Aidan give her just enough for her to forget the death of her boyfriend, Francis. I didn't want her to suffer." I grabbed up the bottle and guzzled down a healthy dose.

"Instead, it killed her?" The Cajun finished my sentence.

I grinned bitterly. "I was told by a questionable source that it was Aidan's adopted sister, Helen, who finished my mother off. But that little fact didn't help my case any. I still got charged for three deaths. My mom and two of her boyfriends.

"Merde! Did you do time?"

"Yep! They sent me up the river to an insane asylum."

The Cajun began coughing again over his drink. Finally, when his scratchy voice returned, he asked, "Are you guilty *and* insane?" Surprise siphoned the color from his face.

"Nope, I'm innocent. Van, Aidan's uncle, and a legion of Illuminist, set me up. Once I gave birth to my child, they didn't feel threatened any longer. So, they released me."

"*Merde!* You are mighty young to have been through such a turbulent life."

"I'm a survivor," I shrugged. "What about you? What do you do for a living before our world was jerked out from under us?"

"Moi!" he grinned to himself. "Contrary to popular belief, I happen to be a doctor. My *grand mere* instilled that in me. She practiced medicine in the unconventional way. She worked with herbs and magic potions for healing."

"Really! My neighbor dealt in the same stuff. She once read my future." A sudden sting of heartburn struck. "My neighbor warned me about Aidan.

The Cajun laughed. "Hell! Even I could've seen that coming."

I smiled but it was burdened with sadness. "Yeah, I was easily fooled back then." I shifted my eyes away. "I liked your grandmother. Even though I had met only her ghost. She was very intuitive and seemed to know things before I had a clue," I smiled.

"Oui! I was taken aback when you delivered her message. I'd been a bad grandson. I should've painted her house." A faint light twinkled in the depth of his black eyes.

"I remember," I laughed softly.

Then the Cajun abruptly changed the direction of our light conversation. "He's your first, yes?"

Why did he go there of all people? I

answered begrudgingly, "Yes, first of everything. In the beginning, I fought my feelings. I knew he'd break my heart. I just didn't realize the magnitude. It's quite terrifying when your life is taken away and you've lost everyone you ever loved."

His mouth curved into an unconscious smile. "I can't imagine you afraid of anything."

"Are you kidding!" I snorted. "I'm afraid of my own shadow. In fact, I am petrified." I grabbed the bottle back and took a huge gulp.

"That sounds pretty human to me."

I grinned, wiping my mouth with the back of my hand. "Yeah, that's what I keep telling myself."

For a minute reticence fell between us as we passed the Jack Daniels between us.

Then I asked, "That night at the barbeque when we first met... why did you kiss me?" I glanced down at the bottle. My cheeks flushed.

"I thought you needed to be kissed by a real man," he laughed to himself. "*Non!* The real truth is that I thought you were beautiful, full of fire that I couldn't resist the temptation."

When he handed the bottle back to me, I paused gripping the bottleneck, "And now you hate me?"

"*Non!*" he shook his head, brows colliding

into a furrow. "I don't hate you," he smiled. "I rather admire you. To be so young, you're a brave soldier. I'd be proud to serve with you."

"Really?" Suddenly, I glanced up meeting his eyes.

"You have heart and courage," his soft browns searched longingly into my gaze. I sat there still in the moment as the Cajun leaned toward me, his eyes filled with tenderness.

I froze, uncertain of what to do.

Startled by a loud clatter from outside. We both froze. Robotic voices sounded angry and agitated. The Cajun and I both vaulted to our feet and sprinted to the front door. He leaned against the wall by the door and I stood across on the other side. He'd cocked his pistol, gripping it in both hands. My magickal daggers were out, hovering over my shoulder and ready for attack. We both listened intently. Neither one of us at that moment dared to breathe.

After a few seconds, we heard heavy footsteps. My horrified eyes locked with the Cajun's. With alarm strapped to our boots, we didn't have to guess who was making the ruckus. The *regulators* were pillaging through our Jeep. *Crap!* If they took our ride, we were screwed.

In a blink of an eye our dilemma exploded. The Cajun decided to do a James Bond move. Without warning, he hit the doors, ducking, and rolling, firing his gun.

I lurched to my feet, staying on the Cajun's heels with my daggers ready for action. I ran for cover behind the light post. In a flash, gunfire went off... *Bang! Bang! Bang!* Shots blasted in my ears.

Unable to see past the dark smoke and shadows, the Cajun's voice pierced the murk, calling my name. Then silence devoured all sound. An eerie silent shifted the air. Before I knew it, three regulators were right on top of us, firing back at both Nick and me. The creatures' weapons far surpassed our technology. The Cajun and his small pistol didn't have a chance against their high-power weaponry.

All of a sudden, I heard a loud humming like a swarm of bees. I looked up to the dark sky and spied three objects that appeared to operate on their own cognizance, intelligence of the fourth kind. They appeared similar to the drones we saw earlier. They were made of some unknown substance that reminded me of molten metal. The strange drones had no solid form. They were clear like a bubble and their shape kept changing like liquid.

One spotted me and hummed to the other drones. It was communicating. In less than a blink, its silver shine grew into a flaming ball of fire. One of my knives shot up and pierced the center of the thing. It sputtered with a fight, fluttering like a butterfly dipping up and down. It finally lost its power, crashing to the ground, exploding, and shooting sparks in every direction. I ducked behind a trashcan but ended up struck as I cried in silence from the sheer burn.

I no more caught my breath when I spotted a speedy missile soaring straight for me. I hit the ground, but the missile still charged at me. It was as though it had some kind of sensor. Quickly, I bolted for cover as the missile stayed hot on my tail. It was only inches from blowing me to smithereens. I dove into the alleyway right before the missile crashed into the corner of the building. A huge chunk of brick and mortar exploded, shattering into a powdery dust. I hid behind a bin that spilled with decaying trash. I was in luck. I think the stench threw off the missile as it returned to the regulators.

I sat there for a second trying to calm my

trembling nerves. As much as I wanted to find cover and hide, I knew I had to get to Nick.

Trembling with unsteady legs, I got to my feet and carefully peered around the corner. *Damn!* The regulators had the Cajun, kicking him viciously as he lay there on the concrete sidewalk helplessly. Those damn bullets he fired only irritated the creatures. I watched as sweat beaded across my forehead and my hands shook like a three-day-old drunk. I couldn't just stand here and watch. The regulators were brutally torturing the Cajun, leaving him in his own pool of blood while they took turns kicking the crap out of him. With each forceful blow, his body rose up off the ground. If I didn't act fast, he wouldn't last long.

I had my knives tucked behind me. I didn't want them spotted. Taking a deep breath for courage, I stepped out into the wide open. "Hey!" I yelled sauntering down the sidewalk encroaching upon them. "It's not fair three against one!" A smirk played across my face as I spread my arms a part daring them. "Come fight a Zop!" I taunted. Funny, when they heard the word " Zop" they all three stopped and turned their reptile eyes on me. They knew my race and a sense of pride came over me.

"That's right you, *circle-jerks*, I'm part of the Zophasmin race." I flashed a seedy grin.

The big one spoke out, "It's because of you, angel, that we lost five of our kind," he snarled. "You must pay for your crimes!" The three regulators started growling and hissing like animals. Eeriness ignited through me.

I acted on instinct, calling to my essence and it answered with glee. The regulators pointed their weapons at me and fired. This time, I deflected the deadly missiles, thrusting my palms out. To my disbelief, the bombs ricocheted off me as if an impenetrable barrier stood between me and the missiles.

The regulators halted, reptile eyes widened with astonishment. That was when I swung into action. Quickly, I ordered my magickal daggers to attack. Upon command, they soared through the air, whizzing past me, hilt over blade, with perfect precision until they stopped with fatal impact, ramming its deadly blade through each lizards' skull. The sound of skin and bone cracking wafted into the humid night. Immediately following, sulfur filled my nostrils. I reckoned that was the stench of their blood.

They all spewed blue toxin and screeched like hyenas dropping to the ground with a loud thud. Their bodies seized, limbs thrashing nonsensically and then they stilled, bodies went limp. I counted my lucky stars that they were down. With all the blue liquid puddling around them, I presumed if they weren't dead, they soon would be.

My attention shot to the Cajun as I raced to his side. Fear pulled through me, terrified that I might be too late. I slid to my knees, urgently placing my index finger and my middle finger over his carotid artery. He laid too still on the concrete with his knees drawn to his chest in a fetal position. "Nick! Get up! *Now!*" I shook him. His eyes popped open and started to swing at me, but as soon as he realized it was me, he calmed. "Come on we have to get moving," I tugged at him.

"*Non!* You go. I'm dying. I'll slow you down," he insisted in a faltering voice.

"Like hell, soldier! Get your ass up!" I commanded. I reckoned that I'd made a believer out of him. Even though I saw the consuming pain in his face, he managed to get to his feet with my assistance, leaning heavily on me for support. Half dragging the Cajun, we made it to the Jeep. I helped him into the passenger seat, belted him in and with no time left, I dove for the driver's side. I snatched the keys from my pocket and motioned for my daggers to return to their sheath.

In a matter of seconds, I floored that Jeep in reverse, wheels bouncing off three large lumps. They were still down from the knife wounds and hopefully the tires would flatten their faces. We wasted no time hauling ass heading for the outskirts of the city.

Every minute counted. No telling how many regulators overheard the commotion. I could hear their cannons miles away. And even worse, those three knew who we were. I had a strong hunch the others knew about us too. The odds weren't in our favor.

The moonshine and homemade bombs had a fatal reaction to their internal organs. Ultimately, we were the cause of the regulators' death. I reckoned after our baleful act of rebellion, the Illuminati would be sicking their posse on the Cajun and me. One good thing that we knew for certain was that our homemade concoctions worked. That brought a smile to my face.

Since the stars and moon weren't out, we were steeped in darkness. According to Toe, there was a curfew. The regulators patrolled the streets at night. I felt like we were rolling into a minefield. I took extra care to keep my eyes open as we tore through the city heading for refuge. Wherever that might be. One thing I did know was that we needed to find shelter and fast.

By the Cajun's pale face and pasty lips, he was in serious trouble. I think he had passed out rather than fallen asleep. I could tell he was still breathing by the slight rise and fall of his chest. But his breathing was shallow, meaning he was growing weaker by the minute.

I had high hopes that certain abilities that Aidan acquired might've been bestowed upon me. *His healing.* I didn't know how to activate that skill, but I had to find a way to tap into the ability. I couldn't let Nick die on my behalf.

I bit my lip to feel pain. *Anything but the guilt that riddled my entire body.* If I'd listened to Nick, he wouldn't have gotten hurt and we wouldn't be running for our lives. I had tunnel vision. All that pummeled my mind was saving Jeffery and Dom. My one-mindedness caused harm to the Cajun. The sting in my eyes stole my breath. I shouldn't have played the moral card on him. It was unfair of me to hold him to his promise. I think that after I heal him and he gets back on his feet, we should part ways. I'd search for the guys on my own. I made a wrong call coercing the Cajun to come with me. I needed to apologize, but first, I needed to get us out of the city and on a dark backroad where we would be out of harm's way.

All of a sudden, an idea struck.

RESPITE

*B*y the skin of my derrière, we made it out of the city limits without a hitch. Well, not entirely. The left tire whined against the road as it grew flat. The turbulent ride burdened me with dread. Regardless, we were pointed straight for Aidan's place. Hell or high water, I wasn't giving up. I kept telling myself that we had only a little farther to go.

Sally spoke of Aidan owning a historical mansion down on the river road. She described it as a shroud of trees lining the drive that led to a huge white plantation.

I reckoned that I'd stay with the Cajun until he was strong enough to fend for himself and then I think we should separate. But first things first, we both needed food and drink and sleep. Alcohol wasn't my idea of nourishment, but the Cajun might beg to differ.

Another thing to add to the list was finding gasoline. The Jeep was running on fumes. If I didn't find some, the Cajun and I'd be walking. I hated to think about being on foot and trying to stay out of sight. It was hard enough out running a regulator in the Jeep. When my angel abilities worked, my chances were slightly higher escaping the regulators, but my powers were unreliable.

The Cajun seemed quite agile on that attack earlier, but he wasn't fast enough or strong enough to out fist them. God forbid that we get gang-banged by several of those dirty bastards. The Cajun and I on foot would be like committing suicide. I'd worry about that after I get him well. That was if I could invoke that power.

The uprising had just begun, and I dared not to think about how bloody our world would become. The Illuminati didn't care about the afflictions they were imposing. Mankind, had nowhere to escape. The human race was doomed. No clean water or medicine for the sick. Food was scarce. And there was no one strong enough, fierce enough that could stand up against them. This world as we once knew it was facing distinction. Hell, the dinosaurs, and Neanderthals all perished. Mankind could face the very same ending too.

I saw exactly what was going on here. The Illuminati intended to take the world by sweeps and bounds, letting innocent people die a slow agonizing death. This heinous act of ridding the world of the underprivileged and replacing those poor souls with super-humans, superior genetic humans, made me ill. They were creating a perfect race. Historians say that history repeats itself. This sounded much like a worldwide *Hitler on steroids*.

I glanced at the Cajun and my heart sunk. He came to protect me. Boy, did he bite off more than he could chew! Now he lay quiet, dying. And if he expired, I had only myself to blame. He was a noble man even with his flaws. I understood now why Val entrusted him. Sadly, Val didn't think about how dangerous it was placing me in the care of a mortal. Anyone who hangs with me was facing a death sentence. What was Val thinking?

I threw my cap off my head, tossing it in the

back of the Jeep and raked my fingers roughly through my dirty hair. Geez! What I wouldn't do for a hot shower and a cold beer? I snorted to myself. I hated beer. Yet it seemed so… *normal*. Crap! I craved normal. My gut told me this was the new norm. Running, starving, dirty, dressed in rags, destitute and homeless. A new kind of indigent.

This was no life for anyone. My heart ached for the people and their families. The *children*. Oh my God! What about the children? I needed to find a way to fight this atrocity. I couldn't give up. If I was supposed to save the world because, after all, I was a genetically altered angel, I should have the ability and a sound plan to take my world back! But the truth was I was useless and that made me furious. If that wasn't being human, then what was?

My mind went back to that day on Bourbon Street. The people standing in the food line. Their faces withdrawn and void. No expression, just blank. They looked more like the walking dead than the living. No glimmer of light or twinkle in their eyes, brain-dead at its best. I knew there was a connection to that ink number six six six stamped on their wrist. I felt it deep in my gut that somehow the

Illuminati concocted a way to control the masses of people by inserting a mind-controlling implant through the ink. How else were they keeping people under their dominance? The thought of how far the Illuminati would go disturbed me on so many levels. I knew this uprising promised only havoc and bloodshed. The Illuminist, sadistic, cold murdering bastards, was seizing the human world. Mankind didn't have a chance against their advance technology. Humans were sitting ducks.

As we came around the bend, I spotted the house just ahead, a huge Victorian house with towering pillars and the house painted white as snow. This had to be it... *Aidan's plantation.* I glanced at the Cajun. He hadn't made a peep since we made our get-away. I saw that he was still breathing. Relief washed over me. I still had a chance in healing him. I felt hopeful.

I came to a slow speed and turned down the long drive. In spite of our dire situation, I gasped at the unwavering beauty. Sally didn't exaggerate. The drive leading up to the mansion offered a thick green canopy of majestic oaks. The land was an endless carpet of plush green. The home sat front and center commanding attention in its glory of the old South. It dominated the graceful grounds just like any master. It had huge columns connected with wrought iron. Long narrow windows covered with plantation shutters lined the front porch and balcony. Black wicker chairs sat elegantly on the porch as if they were waiting for guest to arrive. The home had to have been over a hundred years old yet, it stood just as mighty. I didn't expect anything less.

We cautiously rolled down to the end of the drive, halting at the front steps of the mansion. After I killed the car, I waited for any signs of life. The old place was as still as a haunted house. The cluster of trees rustled loudly through the warm breeze and a faint smell of crepe myrtle perfumed the air. I drew in a deep whiff. God, how I missed that scent.

The house was pitch black. No porch light or the flicker of a candle inside nor out. Most locals didn't have electricity but then again this was Aidan's house. As I spied over the grounds, it suggested to me that we were the only living souls at this grand home. But I wasn't quite sold on that just yet.

I went straight for the door taking two steps at a time up the stairs. I stopped at the entrance staring at a brass bell off to the side. It looked like it was attached to a mechanical device leading into the house. I reached up and pulled down on the rope and off to the side of the door. I stood there against the wall as the bell sounded off. I made sure it was loud enough for anyone in the house to hear. The echo of the bell assured me it made its rounds throughout the house announcing our arrival. Still, the house remained silent.

I decided to check the back. I jumped off the side of the porch and headed in that direction quietly. The backyard was just as lovely as the front. Azaleas and sweet smelling crepe myrtle embellished the yard with lawn chairs placed about the garden. Several windows lined the back of the house. I peeked through one window that appeared to be the kitchen, in another window I spotted a long table with chairs. Still, no sign of life. Good! The easiest way to break in would be through the sunroom. I looked around double checking if the coast was clear. I held my hand to the knob and concentrated. The door gave just as it did at Val's apartment.

To my surprise, there was no alarm sounding off. A sigh of relief hit, and I thought just maybe we might be safe here. Or at least for the night. I cautiously stepped through the threshold holding my breath. I decided to do a final walk-through just to be safe. One could never be too careful.

After I felt confident that we were alone, I went out the front to get the Cajun. He hadn't awakened but he still was breathing. I nudged him to try to get him stirring. I knew I couldn't carry him up those stairs. "Hey! Soldier, wake up!" I demanded. I slightly shook him. I knew the pain would stir him enough that I could get him awake and on his feet. Finally, he started to move. He groaned gritting his teeth. "Where are we?"

I figured the less he knew the better. "Come on! I need to get you in the house."

"*Non!* Leave me!" he grumbled nearly passing out again.

"Soldier, I'm not asking. Get your ass up! You can do this," I promised.

Slowly, he moved one leg at a time and after a few French curse words flying from his mouth, he was standing on his feet. I threw his arm around my neck, we ventured our way up the steps and into the house.

I lay him down on the sofa in a room to the left. It looked like some sort of fancy parlor with a grand piano in the corner. The sofa looked like it came from the same century of the house. The whole house with its high ceilings and crystal chandeliers carried the same Victorian vibe, even the wallpaper. Strange, I thought. This room didn't fit Aidan at all. Of course, there were a lot of things about him that didn't seem like him.

Once I got the Cajun settled and comfortable, I rushed to hide the Jeep. I didn't want anyone spotting us from the road. I raised the garage door that was on the backside of the house. To my surprise, a Hummer sat parked nicely polished as if it were ready for a long trip. In spite of the size of the truck, the centuries old garage had enough room for the Jeep. I thought after I took care of the Cajun, I'd come back out here and check this place out. No telling what I might find useful.

Once I'd tucked the Jeep away and closed the garage door, I rushed back in the house to the Cajun. I checked his pulse and felt relieved that he was still breathing; but his condition was becoming dire. His breath was stressed, and his coloring had grayed. I glanced around looking for a lamp but then I remembered we couldn't use any lights. The last thing I needed was alerting unsavory characters to our presence. I had to do this magickal task in the dark. I just hoped I didn't slice him in two since I'd never performed this procedure. That was if I could figure how to get my hand to glow. But if my memory served me right, whatever magickal talents Aidan possessed, I too carried through my veins.

I looked down at his swollen face. I didn't have to be a physician to know that time was running out. The Cajun wasn't going to make it through the night unless I intervened. I took a deep breath trying to calm my trembling hands. I kneeled down beside the Cajun as he lay flat on the couch. I eased my hands on his chest and closed my eyes focusing. My mind wouldn't settle. It felt like a freight train going from zero to ninety. And worse, my essence appeared empty. I sensed nothing. My heart rate kicked up several notches like a fluttering hawk clawing to escape.

I stretched my neck and eased my breathing for the second time. Slowly, I exhaled and inhaled. I did this for several seconds to rest my mind and body. Then I called to my essence and with promise, it answered. This time as I had never experienced, it appeared gentle and soft as a white dove. Slowly, it feathered its way to the surface. I opened my eyes and surprise consumed me as a bright glow radiated from my hand. It was warm like a blanket spreading its mystical caress throughout the Cajun's body.

I focused on its soothing touch and after a few minutes, his eyes popped open with a gasping breath. Startled, I jumped back, gaping at my glowing hands then back at the Cajun, jolted to a sitting position.

"What did you do to me?" he demanded as his voice came in short pants and raspy as his eyes flew open gawking at my hands.

"I-I'm not sure. How do you feel?"

"Better!" he half-laughed, raising his shirt and rubbing his stomach. "The pain is mild." his eyes were gentle but confused.

"Okay, that's good!" I slowly breathed. "Let me finish." I sat up on my knees, back in position. "Hold still." I reckoned since my hands were still glowing and he wasn't completely out of pain, I still needed to do some more work. I steadied my hands on his stomach as I held my eyes on the focal point. The glow coursed through me as well and spilled over onto the injured area of the Cajun's abdomen.

After the glow faded, I sat back pulling my hands to my chest. "All right, all done, I think."

I held my breath fretting that I might've over done it.

The Cajun slowly opened his eyes as our gaze met. "I'm better." He started to rise.

"No, don't get up!" I urged with my hand pushing his shoulder back down.

"You truly are *moi ange!*" (My angel) The Cajun stared at me with awe.

"I-I guess so." My face flushed.

Our eyes locked and his fingers clamped down on my trembling chin. The expression in his current black eyes seemed to plea for something that I'd never seen in him before. "Thank you," he half whispered.

It felt as if he could see every rotten last bit of me. I didn't deserve his gratitude. His near death was my fault. "I don't deserve your gratitude. You nearly died because of me."

"Why do you say that?"

"I coerced you into coming. If I'd not been so determined to go back, you'd be off on the river safe."

"Gul! You didn't trick me into coming. I came because I'd rather be with a beautiful woman than alone with the mosquitoes and gators," he flashed a weak smile. "Now I got to witness a miracle. It was worth the injury."

"I'm happy you're going to live," I smiled

back. Taking a deep, unsteady breath, I quickly changed the subject, glancing down at my hands. "Wow! I have the gift," I giggled staring down at my hands, amazed.

He leaned back on the couch, fitting his fingers together, resting them over his chest. "You didn't know?"

"No," I shook my head. "I never had the opportunity to test it."

"Do angels like you usually have this gift?"

"Val has the ability. He used it on me once but not at this magnitude," I paused, as pain wedged in my throat. I hated memory lane. "This might sound bizarre but I think I inherited this power from Aidan."

"Aidan!" The Cajun nearly croaked on his words.

"Can you be still?" I snapped, taking my hand, gently pushing him back down on the couch.

"*Désolé.* (Sorry), I am stunned. How did this happen?" His brows drew together in disbelief.

Oh geez! I wasn't sure I wanted to drag out my whole life. I had enough demons to fill my brain already. I sighed. "It's a long story." I fiddled with my hands, avoiding eye contact.

"I got time. Tell me," the Cajun insisted.

"Hmm, before I was born, our families

made arrangements for Aidan and me to marry."

"*Merde!*" the Cajun snarled his lips. "Marriage with the devil himself? I thought those kinds of arrangements were a thing of the past, *no?*"

"One would assume," I grimaced. "I'm not sure how to say this but my father was once a member of the Illuminati."

The Cajun's glint held incertitude as his mouth opened and closed. Before he uttered a word, I protested, holding my palm up. "Let me explain," I said. "My father left the Family, leaving behind their political beliefs, their harsh traditions. He left behind that world and everything in it including the wealth."

"That had to be hard, leaving behind his entire life." The Cajun marveled as if it was some impossible feat.

It almost was.

"My father was more of a humanitarian. He didn't approve of the Illuminati's sadistic ways. So, I reckoned that he rebelled by taking a shine to a worldly person, an outsider, my mother, Sara. As the story churns, he eloped with my mom."

"Ah, nothing like young love, yes?"

I flinched, remembering how Sara told her

side of the story, the viciousness in her voice. It was worse than hoards of rocks hurling at my body. "Well, their marriage wasn't exactly a fairytale."

"Your *mère* must've had great admiration for your father standing up to that sadistic family, yes?"

"No, Sara wasn't the type to think outside the box. Instead, she had an ulterior motive. My mom agreed to marry my father because of his wealth. Sara wanted a life of luxury. Her dreams soon were shot down on the night of their honeymoon. It was not until then that my father revealed his truth; he was penniless for the first time in his life. Sara hated him for that. And for his betrayal, she decided she would get revenge. Sara stayed married to my father, but she wasn't exactly a model wife."

The Cajun laughed bitterly. "Eh, loose women! They take from you until you have nothing else to give and then poof!" He brought his fingers to his lips, making a kissing sound. "They leave," he smirked.

"It sounds like you're talking from experience," I half laughed.

"*Oui!* I am twenty-nine. I have a few bumps in the way. I loved a girl once. She damn near broke my heart." His eyes drifted off as if his thoughts were revisiting a past he'd forgotten.

"I'm sorry to hear that."

"It was a long time ago. I am over it. Maybe a scar or two, eh!" he shrugged.

"It seems that getting jilted by a lover runs strong in my family," I huffed before I continued. "Unfortunately, my father didn't see Sara for her true self. As the miscarriages continued, Sara pretended that she was devastated over losing a baby. It was all a con."

"This just gets worse."

"That's not the half of it. The Family had a watchful eye on my parents and knew about Sara abusing herself. Someone from the Family approached her offering a deal."

The Cajun scoffed. "A deal with the devil, yes?"

"Yup. That's how I came into the picture. To sum it all up, the Illuminati's scientist, with the assistance of alien technology, was able to use a celestial being's DNA and my human father's to create me… *a genetically engineer angel.*"

The Cajun rose up on his elbows, gawking at me before he'd found his tongue. "That's impossible!"

I dragged in a wary sigh. "Alien technology

has mankind beat hands down. I'm the proof," I smiled bitterly.

"That is very interesting. So, how did your birth and the Illuminati come into play?"

"That's the easy part. My parents signed a blood contract with the Family. There was a two-fold agreement to the contract that my mother and the Family made together in secret. She would exchange me to my betrothed once I turned the ripe age of eighteen. That's when my mother and I moved to Tangi."

"What happened to your father?"

"Dad died by a hit-and-run driver, my mother. She managed to hide that little fact from me until after I'd met Aidan. He was the one who sprang it on me."

"Mère! That must have shattered your world."

"It did but that was only the tip of the iceberg. Aidan kindly took the time to explain the history of my family, and he's the one who told me about myself. I didn't believe him at first, but it all made sense in a really crazy screwed up way."

"Non! You mean to tell me that you trusted that sociopath at his word. He's a murderer!" the Cajun grinded his words between his teeth.

"Hmm, it wasn't like that in the beginning.

Aidan was very different. He was dashing, strong, tender, and intense." I shuddered inwardly remembering the past. "He was protective of me and I fell in love with him." I shrugged, unable to say any more.

"He doesn't sound like the jackass I know."

"The Aidan I once knew, and the present Aidan are polar opposites." I licked my dry lips. "That's why I think his family has him under some sort of enchantment."

"How did you inherit his powers?"

"I was being hunted down by his uncle, Edward Van Dunn. He wanted to extract my powers for himself."

"The same pervert that asshole, Aidan bragged about?"

"Yup, that would be the same psychopath that wanted my head on a platter," I sighed. "Anyway, to protect myself and to keep Aidan safe, I offered myself to him. It involved me losing my virginity."

"Damn! He tricked you!"

"Yes, it seems so, doesn't it?" I forced a smile. "I thought he cared." I scoffed, remembering the pain of betrayal.

"Did he have anything to do with you going to that insane hospital?"

"I believe so. He didn't come completely

clean. He has selective amnesia. Aidan has a problem remembering certain things that went down back then."

"It doesn't matter. He's a monster." The Cajun's face soured.

"I have to agree." I shook my head, frustrated. "Could I have been that blind?"

"Love is a funny emotion. You could fall for an axe murderer and not see the truth."

"I reckon you're right."

"Pardon me, but I overheard you say something about a girl named Dawn."

Tears welled into my eyes as I quickly dabbed them dry with my sleeve. "Yes, Dawn is mine and Aidan's daughter. She was murdered by a dark angel that I share the other DNA with, and I have a blade with his name on it." I swallowed down the vile that threatened.

"You lost your child! No wonder you are bitter."

The Cajun had me pegged right.

"First chance I get, I'm going after him too. He will pay for what he's done." My lips tightened into anger.

"This is the angel you are related to?"

"I share only Mustafa's DNA. Nothing else."

"I certainly can relate to that emotion. I

wish revenge for my friend too. But first comes first."

"Meaning?"

"Meaning, you don't show up for a gun fight with a knife. You be patient until you get the upper hand. Then you attack."

"That sounds like you're speaking about your tour in the middle East."

"*Oui!* I lost good men." Quiet settled between us, and then he switched to another uncomfortable subject. "What happened to Valor and you? I thought you two were tight."

"Oh, Val!" I half laughed. "Yeah, it didn't work out."

"I apologize if my kissing you caused you to part ways."

I laughed. "Don't flatter yourself, Cajun. No. I'm afraid there were other factors that played into our breakup." I looked down at my hands, feeling heavy hearted. "He was the leader of my kind, Zophasemin. Although I am the same race, I'm marked as an impure and an outcast."

"Ouch! That must've hurt?"

"It did hurt very much and is still raw."

"I gather he chose his kind."

"Yep! You gathered right."

He drew his brows down into a puzzled gaze. "Why are you an outsider?"

I huffed, feeling the bite of ire. "I'm not a creature of divine creation. I was created by a team of scientist that were handpicked by the Illuminati."

"*Merde*! That explains why those bastards are hunting you."

I shrugged, looking down at my lap. "Yep, I'm not even my own person," I sighed. "That's why Val and I broke up. I'd never be accepted by the Zop."

The Cajun snorted. "It's his lost, yes?" his lips tipped up, hinting at a smile.

"Perhaps. I don't know anymore. I thought I loved him but when we broke up, I wasn't that unhappy. Of course, I didn't like him leaving earth's realm. When I heard he was leaving, it was like a cold slap in the face. I thought I stilled loved him but then..."

The Cajun jumped in. "You don't miss him so much?"

"No, I'm more upset at him for leaving the people than for myself. He should be here protecting defenseless folks."

"He's doing what he thinks is best."

"Maybe or maybe not." I rose to my feet. I'd had a belly full of my past. "You need to eat and no liquor tonight. You need your strength."

"What? I'm perfectly fine. See?" He raised his shirt. The deep bruises had faded but I remembered how I felt when Aidan had healed me from a fatal wound. I was putting my foot down. "Sorry! One night doing without liquor won't hurt you. I'm going to find us something to eat." I threw over my shoulder as I headed for the kitchen. "Don't move off that couch!" I ordered before I disappeared to the back.

The kitchen felt like a mixture of old and contemporary. Chrome shelves with an old wooden stove and a stack pipe going through the ceiling. Exposed stone embellished the mantle and fireplace. When I spotted the stainless-steel fridge, my eyes lit up.

Good question if the house had electricity. If I flipped on a light switch, it could be a beacon in the dark. Drawing attention to ourselves could get us caught. We were already on borrowed time. No point in pushing the bounds of luck any further.

I reached around the back and felt for the plug. Once my fingers band around the cord, I gave it a brisk tug. "There!" I huffed, tugging the door open.

My breath stalled as I stood there swooned

with crisp cold air caressing my face. Surprise and glee surged through me as my mouth began to water. I hadn't eaten since yesterday morning. It seemed luck had our backs for now.

Right off, I spotted orange juice, milk, eggs, and cold cuts for sandwiches with all the trimmings too, tomatoes and pickles. I overloaded my arms with all the goodies and placed them on the counter. Then I went to the pantry and my eyes widened with delight. I spotted bread, cookies, canned soup, and bottled water. I figured when we got ready to leave, I'd help myself to the staples that didn't need refrigeration. Too bad all that food we'd gathered at Val's apartment got wasted. The regulators ruined all our findings, smashing it all over the sidewalk. They knew it was food. I reckoned the New World Order only allowed folks to eat food they provided. Whata bunch of dickweeds. The cynicism of this new world grated on me furiously. But for now, we had shelter and food. That was more than what most had. I was grateful.

I opened a can of chicken soup for the Cajun. I hustled about the kitchen as though it was my own. A few minutes later, I came out with a tray of sorted foods.

The Cajun was sitting up, but he still looked a little under the mend. I fretted if I'd completed the healing process completely. Now that I knew I had the touch, literally speaking, I'd keep my eye on him. Apart from his slight paleness, he looked pretty good. Maybe we both can get a few hours of sleep.

I set the tray on the floor next to the sofa where the Cajun sat. I grabbed up his bowl of hot soup and eased down next to him. "The soups hot." I blew a moment and raised the spoon to him. His eyes gleamed with amusement. I stopped in midair, I asked, "What?"

"Nothing. Just never expected to see you feed me. That's all."

"Do you want to feed yourself? Or better, you could wear it?" I replied letting the scorn flavor my voice a little too heavy.

"*Non*. It's fine. You do it." Sarcasm dipped in his deep throaty voice like a cookie to coffee.

I hesitated a second and thought what the hell, he'd nearly lost his life for me. I owed him a lot more than a spoon-feeding, but I did have my limits. "Alright, but you can't tease me." I shot him a smothering look. I raised the spoon back to his lips and he took the sip.

"Good!" he whispered and flashed a devilish smile.

Time ticked away as an old grandfather clock chimed throughout the mansion. We sat there in the dark not speaking. By the drained look in the Cajun's face, I was certain that my face parroted his. The night had devoured us both. Despite the odds, he was going to live or at least for now. I put myself in the same statistics as well. Nothing was stable and any hope of a future in this new system was bleak.

After tonight, the Cajun and I should part ways. I couldn't have him lose his life for me. Though my angel gifts were unreliable, I had an advantage. That was more than the Cajun.

Nick knew the land. He could hunt or trap just about any wild creature on the bayou. He was a survivor. I knew if he went deep into the back woods, down the river, he could hide, and no one would ever find him.

Then again with alien technology and those eerie drones, no telling what sort of satellite they had spying on us lowly ones.

Regardless of the advanced tech, he had a better chance surviving in the bayou than hanging with me. I, on the other hand, didn't have that luxury. I had to find the guys. Then after they were tucked away in a safe place, I was turning myself over to the Illuminati. The Cajun and his friends along with Dom and Jeffery, didn't need me hanging on their shirttails. I was a liability. Besides, it was only a matter of time before the Illuminati's dogs found me. My going off in the opposite direction might throw off the Cajun's scent and make it easier for him to get away. It was a theory, but it was all I had for the time being.

After we'd finished eating, the Cajun grumbled about the OJ. "What no liquor in the juice?" he scowled with uttered contempt.

My furrowed brows met his scowl as I responded, "Will you just shut up and be grateful you have a full belly? You don't need liquor with every meal!"

"I'm a big boy. I think I can decide for myself," he shot back with his nostrils flaring.

I dragged in a long sigh and figured it wasn't worth blowing up over. Instead I said, "If you want to destroy your liver, I reckon that's your right."

The Cajun's face dropped, full of regret. "I'm sorry. That was rude of me."

"You, rude? Never!" I flashed him a seedy grin.

"Okay, I deserved that," he paused, "You and me, we're gonna make it, yes?"

"Your guess is as good as mine," I said. "But I think it's best that we part ways after tonight." I suddenly felt a tug of sadness.

He eased himself down to the floor next to me. His body moved stiffly as he grimaced. I avoided his eyes. I just didn't want him to see me fragile like this. We both had lost so much, his best friend, my mother and Dawn, my child, now the guys. How much more torture did we have to bear?

For a moment, we didn't say anything to each other as we leaned against the sofa taking in the darkness. I stared off at the empty fireplace remembering the inviting warmth. On cold nights, Dom would throw in a few pinecones on top of the burning wood. I'd never forget that wonderful scent of pine floating throughout the house. I wished I could go back in time. If I had a day to choose, I'd pick a time before Dawn's death. Maybe I could've prevented it. Then I sighed. She'd be growing up in this terrible mutiny. The world as it was, certainly no place to raise a child. Could death have been a blessing? My eyes suddenly felt the onset of tears. I fought the sting. No parent should ever have to lose a child. What was wrong with this world?

"Are you crying?" the Cajun's voice roped me back in.

I released a wary sigh. "No." I avoided his penetrating eyes.

"I have a nice shoulder to cry on."

I almost giggled. Why did the Cajun have to be nice to me of all nights? While focusing on a flaw in the plank flooring to keep my eyes from finding his, I retorted, "It doesn't matter now!" I swallowed hard. Damn knot wouldn't go away.

"You and I will find your boys, and everything will be fine."

Sorrow spilled from my smile. "Nick, I can't have you tag along anymore." He opened his mouth to protest but I stopped him, holding my fingers to his lips. "Look, I know you're trying to comfort me and," I swallowed. "That's sweet but we both know it's too dangerous. I have a target on my back."

"I think after trip 2 to downtown, I'm pretty sure I have the same target, yes?"

I could feel the heat of his eyes on me. "Not like me. I think you can stay under radar, deep in the bayou. I can give you directions where to find Val's cabin. It's completely enshrouded by cypress and gators. Right up your alley."

"I'm not a man that runs from my enemies.

You forget that bastard killed my friend. I want to strangle him with my bare hands."

"A minute ago, you said you never go to a gun fight with a knife. Now you're flip flopping," I accused.

"I didn't say we go running into an enemy territory without a good plan, gul! We strategize, then we go in when they least expect us."

I shook my head. "How do we map out a plan against a druid?" His arrogant tone sparked my frustration. "Look! Your pride is going to get you killed. Aidan can snap you like a twig."

"I know I wanted to hide out at the river. But I was wrong. I gave my word to Valor and I am not backing out!" A chill in his voice stabbed the darkness.

"You saw what he did to Titan. I can't let you risk your life and I don't think your friend would want that for you either."

"I think I know what my friend would want!" The Cajun snapped.

"Okay, you win!" I huffed. "We stay together, then." Geez! There was no reasoning with him. Still, I couldn't blame him. I had my own demons to kill. Mustafa being on the top of my list. One sadistic angel that needed to die. Next on the list was Aidan. I planned to torture him.

~

The Cajun insisted on taking first watch. We stood at an impasse over who watched first. I reckoned it was a man's thing. I didn't argue. Who was I to burst his male pride? I went off scouting out the mansion.

Upstairs, I found the master bedroom at the end of the hall. The room didn't lack in its exquisite décor, a stark white. Although no matter how heavy the price tag, the room felt cold and void. I stood in the center of the large bedroom peering through the darkness. I didn't see anything that had Aidan's stamp on it. Not even that woodsy scent I'd once loved. Instead, the room smelled of rubbing alcohol that stung my nose and eyes. Apparently, someone went to great lengths to sterilize the room for an ill person. There was nothing personal in the bedroom. No pictures of family, no clutter showing evidence of a person using this room, everything was in perfect order. Why would a Druid need his room sterilized? Come to think about it, I'd never seen his private boudoir. A heaviness centered in my chest. I reckoned he reserved that part of his life for Sally.

My eyes fell upon an interior door. I gasped, padding my way through the dark. I stopped at the door and reached for the knob. Slowly, I eased the door open. I peeked inside as I let out a soft whistle. "A shower! And I'm bettin' there's hot water too." I gasped at the white marble. Suddenly my mood lifted.

I quickly peeled off my clothes and stepped into the massive shower. It took me a moment to figure out all the gadgets. "Dang! Why does one need so many knobs for a shower?" I grumbled to myself. Not wasting one moment, I started twisting all the gold knob. Right away, the water heated, shooting warm beads of water. Only moments later, the aroma of gardenias had swept me away. Soon my body was lathered in suds and my world didn't seem as bleak. I stood there letting the pulsating streams beat the dirt and grim down the drain. The tension in my shoulders eased. I stood there breathing in the delicious warmth.

Then my emotions hit me and I suddenly dropped to the floor huddled, racked with sobs. My sense of loss was beyond tears. What had happened to my life? It never really was my life to own. The Illuminati owned me before birth. But there had been so much pain. The loss of a child that I'd never had the privilege to embrace or get to know. My father, murdered before I had a chance to know him, a mother who never truly loved me. And now, my dearest friends, my adopted family, had been kidnapped by a sociopath. Because of my careless mistake, they may be dead. And poor Titan tortured on that satanic cross flashed before my eyes.

Then I thought about Dawn. The tears flooded even more as my whole body shook. I wanted nothing more than death at this point. Maybe if I didn't exist, the world would be less chaotic. The Order wouldn't have someone to chase and others wouldn't be endangered by merely knowing me. An invasion was forced upon our world and I dared to think what the Order planned next. How many innocent lives would have to suffer or die for their greedy rulership? Yet, the worst... I had no power against these fiends. Not only was I useless with my limited magick, I was defenseless against the great mighty and powerful Illuminati. I laid there sobbing until I started choking on my tears. The water had turned cold and I still remained huddled under its icy flow. Chills spurred over my body. Unaware, I heard the shower door open and the cold water ceased. I was shivering, teeth chattering. A shadow moved swiftly as he picked me up with a towel wrapped around me and gently lifted me into his arms. Once I sunk into the cushion of the soft bed, my eyes collided with the Cajun's face. He quickly covered my bare body with the dry covers. Our eyes locked and I suddenly felt a deep appreciation for him. "Did you hear me crying?" I asked.

"*Oui.*" his deep browns glistened in the dark. "Like you... I couldn't abandon you."

Tears began to swell again as my teeth chattered.

"Now take this. You need sleep. I'll continue to watch."

I looked down and the Cajun had a glass of OJ and a tiny pill. My brows furrowed. "What's that?"

"It literally is a chill pill. Xanax. It will help you relax." he held the tiny pink pill up in his hand.

"A narcotic?" I panicked.

The Cajun grinned. "Don't worry. Have you forgotten, I'm a doctor. It is a very low dose. It won't hurt you. I promise."

"Where did you find it?"

The Cajun grinned, "In your bathroom."

"Oh!" I hesitated. I didn't like drugs. Especially after my stay at Haven. Then I thought what the hell. I could use a peaceful rest. I sat up slightly and took the OJ and the pill in my hands. Not wanting to argue, I flipped my head backward, chasing the pill down with the orange juice. "Thanks." I said in a drained voice handing the glass back.

The Cajun smiled, "That's my gul." he paused, "You can't take the whole world on, *non*! You can only save one person at a time. Your heart is good. In my book, that's pretty, damn human!"

I pushed myself to smile but failed miserly. The Cajun seemed to understand and he just patted my foot and left me alone to myself. Once the door creaked shut, I closed my eyes and the tears started flowing once again.

I didn't know how long I'd been dozing, but something jarred me from a dead sleep. I jumped to a sitting position. I let out a sigh of relief when I realized it was only a tree scraping the window. A faint shaft of light peeked through the sheer curtains. Daylight was nearing.

After combing the dim room, it came back to me that we were still in Aidan's house. A frown crept across my face and dread spiked my stomach. I didn't cotton to the idea of staying in his house, even though it was for only a night.

My grogginess had subsided as I sat peering over the room. I tugged the cover off and began to slip out of bed until I realized I didn't have a stitch on. I needed to find something to wear. I imagined Aidan had a belt or two in his closet. I didn't care if the clothes were baggy. A belt could hold the pants up. As long as it didn't fall off my body and it was clean, I'd be happy.

I went straight for the armoire and swung the doors open. Wow! I hit the jackpot. Women's clothing to the galore. "Eureka!" Then a sharp bite slug me in the gut. *Sally!* Could these garments be hers?

A prestigious stock of designer clothing with the tag still attached. My eyes washed over the various brands, Vera Wang, Gucci, Dolce and Gabbana. Strangely, I didn't see any men's clothing. Maybe Aidan stayed in separate quarters. Oh, well! I shrugged it off.

The closet took me back in time when my mother was alive. Sara had a closet very much like this one. I gave way to a somber sigh. Oh well, no time for revisiting the past. It was better buried. I quickly pushed the clothing around trying to find something that was less formal. "Ah, found it!" I pulled out a pair of jeans with holes through the knees and a simple white blouse. I found a pair of black riding boots. I guess this person spent her leisure time riding horses.

I checked the size, a five! Then I thought of Sally. These couldn't be hers unless she'd lost forty pounds. Oh well, like I cared.

I went to the chest of drawers. If Sally or whoever was anything like my mom, she might have undergarments that still had tags. I opened the top drawer and sure enough, I was right! This girl had a ton of panties and bras with tags hanging on the garments. I grabbed up a pair and a pink bra matching. I was in luck, it was my size and brand new. I quickly got dressed. In the bathroom, I found a brush and a hair band. I didn't waste time trying to run a brush through my wild mane of hair so I threw down the brush and tied my hair up in a ponytail.

After a moment of admiring myself in the mirror, I made my way to hallway. Slowly, I creaked the door open, cautiously checking if the close was clear. The house was still dark and quiet. I had no idea the time, but I imagine it would be light soon. We needed to get the hell out of here before anyone noticed us. I tipped toed down the hall opening doors looking for the Cajun.

When I came to one room, I stopped in my tracks. Through the dim light, I recognized the room. It was as if I'd stepped back in time. A time I didn't want to relive... the *principal's office*. I gaped at the room. "Holy crap!" I mumbled barely above a whisper. I shut the door behind me and I made my way to that same ornate desk that I remembered well. Even the scent of tobacco lingered in the room. My gaze combed over the room as if in slow motion taking in every inch of the office.

When my eyes landed on that same ornate desk, I made a beeline for it. I began jiggling the drawers checking for any one unlocked. To my disappointment, the owner had locked it up before leaving.

Then I recalled unlocking Val's apartment door. I wrapped my fingers around a long narrow knob to the master drawer. If I could get into it, the other drawers might automatically open too. I closed my eyes, concentrating. I give it a tug and nothing. It didn't budge. "Dang!" I grated through my teeth. This time I put more will-power onto essence. I tightened my fingers around the metal knob. A light from my palm glistened in the dim light. I tugged harder this time and almost knocked everything off the desk but the knob, itself. It remained steadfast.

Locked!

I flopped back into that god-awful chair. I felt so tiny leaning back in it. I blew out a huff of frustration. My eyes squinted, determination seethe as my mind roiled with ideas. I was breaking into the desk if I had to take a hatchet and chop it into a million pieces. My eyes washed over the top of the desk hoping to find a sharp object. I'd thought about a hair pen. I scratched that idea. If my magick couldn't break it, a thin wire wouldn't work for sure.

I started to swipe everything off the desk in one sweep until my eyes caught the cup holder. A letter opener with a folded note clung to the sharp point, standing erect in the cup.

A seedy smile crossed my face as I jolted up in my seat. I leaned over and snatched the note. My hands were trembling. On the fold, my name was hand written. I froze staring at it. It was the same writing from the note the Cajun and I found lying on his kitchen table from

Aidan. Yet, this writing like the other one was sloppy and looked more like a girl's writing. It had to be Sally's.

I jerked my head up skimming the room. Chills washed over me as if a pair of eyes were watching. Panic seized my breath. The only thing I could hear was my pounding heart. I glanced back down at the folded note. Crap! How did Aidan know that I'd be snooping in his office? My mind flooded with questions that threatened to send me into a tizzy.

I couldn't stand it any longer. I unfolded the note. My hands trembled, barely able to hold the paper steady enough to read. The paper felt soft as a baby's bottom. The color was a starch white with swirls of what appeared to be an eye in an abstract marking, circling the edges of the paper. With a nervous sigh, I began to read:

Dear Stevie,

It is so lovely of you to drop by and visit my home in the country. However, it pains me greatly to inform you that you missed your love ones earlier. Unfortunate for them, you missed a spot. Retract your steps. However, you must hurry. Jeffery and Dom don't have

much time left. They're having a difficult
time breathing, I fear.

Sincerely,
Aidan

Son of a *bitch*! This time I swiped my arm across the surface of the desk, knocking everything off to the floor, crashing. A loud crash burst disturbed the whole house.

I had to find the Cajun! We needed to get the *hell* out of here and fast. I charged out the office with the letter clenched in my hand, yelling down the hall, "Nick! Where are you, *goddamnit!*"

I flew down the stairs darting from room to room searching for him. I halted in the kitchen staring at the coffeemaker brewing. "Well, at least I know he was here a minute ago." I stood resting my hands on my hips huffing in the door jam. Normally, I'd be jonesing over a hot cup of java but my chest was already taking a beating from my heart. I didn't need the caffeine boost.

Obviously, the Cajun was nowhere in the house.

Outside!

I tore out the front door and I spotted the garage door slightly open and a gentle light spilling from underneath. I sprinted toward the garage hoping I'd find the Cajun alive and alone.

I stretched my neck, peering around to see if we had any visitors. I saw nothing out of the ordinary. A slight relief flickered through me, but I remained alert to any surprises just in case.

When I reached the garage door, I needed to make sure the close was clear. One could never be too careful these days. I pressed my back flat against the corner of the building. I stilled, listening over my erratic heartbeat for any signs of the Cajun or unwanted visitors. I heard faint footsteps scrapping across the concrete floor and sounds of metal rubbing against another metal like someone tinkering with a car.

I summed it up in a nutshell and went into action.

I bent down, lifting the door as it squeaked in protest. The Cajun jumped with a start aiming a cocked rifle straight at my head. Looking down the barrel of a gun wasn't what I'd expected from my partner.

As soon as he saw me, curses fell from his mouth, "Gul, I nearly shot you!"

I ignored his canter and blurted out, "We have to leave now! We've been setup. Aidan knows we're here!" frantically, I shoved the letter in his face, "Read this!" Hysteria was banking on the edge of my last strand of sanity. It took all I had to hold myself together.

The Cajun set his rifle down, grabbing the letter from my hand and unfolded it. His eyes quickly scanned over the writing. Dark snappy eyes shot back at me from his sun toughen face. "What does he mean retract our steps? What did we overlook?"

I shifted in my feet and blew out a deep sigh, "Val's gym."

The Cajun stood in silence. His flat unspeaking eyes prolonged the moment. With no warning, he snatched up a screwdriver and hurled it against the wall. It hit the old wood with a vibrating bang, bouncing off and landing on the concrete with a loud ding.

Okay, this was going better than I thought.

"If that no-balls bastard knew we'd end up at his planation, then don't you think us going back to Val's bar is bat-shit crazy? We'll be walking into a trap!" The Cajun shook his head. "*Non!* I think I wish to live, *yes?*"

"That note changes everything! Can't you see that? Dom and Jeffery are still alive. You can stay here if you want, but I'm going back!" Anger had nipped at my heels as I crossed my arms holding my stance.

"I'm not going back there!" the Cajun's voice hinged on the verge of shouting. "And neither are you!"

"Look! I understand your reservations but... "

Abruptly, I stopped in the stream of our argument.

"Phew! What is that awful smell?" I crunched my nose.

The Cajun's glint fixed on an old building farther back on the perimeter of the land. It was such a far distance from the house. I'd over looked it when I'd been scooting out the place last night. There was nothing to it, tattered boards that looked like the wind could knock it down. It was in desperate need of a paint job. Faded red, chipped, exposing boards that were black and rotten. I assumed that it had served as an outhouse back in the day during the planation's early beginnings.

The Cajun as if he'd forgotten about our heated debate, became deathly silent as he stomped off heading for the direction of the shack. His face took on a hunted look and I knew our troubles had changed for the worse.

As we neared the shed, there was a loud buzzing coming from inside. I felt the color drain from my face.

Suddenly, the Cajun stopped right at the door. He'd quickly jerked his bandana over his mouth and nose. When I reached his side, I gagged, quickly covering my mouth. The smell reminded me of decay and lye.

It didn't take a Brainiac to know what laid behind that door. "Oh, my God!" I dropped to my knees. "Nick, please tell me that's not Dom and Jeffery!" Icy fear tore at my insides.

Without a word, the Cajun opened the door. Swarms of buzzing flies flew into his face as he stepped back swatting. The stench of decay attacked the air as we both gagged, covering our faces. Brusquely, the Cajun shut the door and then turned to me. His sorrowful eyes sought mine and sheer panic roared in my eardrums.

"*NO!*" I screeched. "It's not the boys!" Tears clouded my vision. Sheer black terror charged through me. "*Please*, not them!" I pleaded.

"*Non!*" the Cajun rushed to my side, gently lifting me to my feet. "Shush, shush, *cheri!*" I eased in his arms. "*Non!* It's not the boys." His voice was tender. "The body is a woman."

My eyes flew up at him. "A woman?" I asked in a tremulous whisper.

"*Oui*! A young woman."

Suddenly I had to see for myself. I jerked free from the Cajun's embrace and bolted for the door, swinging it open. I quickly stepped back covering my nose and mouth from the horrific stench. "I-I know her!" I stuttered as shock poured over me. Maggots covered her remains, creeping through every crevice, severed body parts tossed into a pile like dog scraps, and thousands of flies blanketed her decomposing body. It was more than sick. It was pure evil.

In a flash, I spun on my heels darting to the side of the shack, bending over, choking up my insides. I swore that I'd coughed up so much vile that my belly was rubbing against my spine. I had no more to give.

The Cajun shut the door to the shack and rushed to my side. I felt his hand pressed against my back, gently stroking. "Who is the *gul*, Stevie?" his voice pierced my madness.

I straightened up tugging out my bandana from my back pocket and cleaning my mouth.

Tears came at me again as I forced the words out. "*Sally!* My cousin and Aidan's wife."

"*Merde!* That psychopath killed his own wife. If you go after him, he will do the same to you or worse."

"Not if I kill him first!" I hissed, squaring my shoulders.

"Did you see her body? He mutilated the gul!" the Cajun flung his arm out, pointing to the shack's door, "I bet that sick fuck had sex with her when he slit her throat."

My stomach roiled over the vision of Sally, now burned forever in my retina. Another death to add to my growing list. "She didn't deserve this!" I looked off staring at the far stretched land. I didn't spot a house in sight. We were in the middle of nowhere. It would've been easy to murder someone here. The screams would've gone unheard. My gaze shot back at the Cajun. "I have to find him!"

"*Non!* You're not going after that cold murdering psychopath!"

"Look! I appreciate your concern. But don't you see the message here?"

The Cajun scoffed. "*Oui!* We get the hell out of dodge."

"I don't have the luxury that you do, just run?" I charged.

"I pick my battles." He grated. "This one is suicide, gul. Your friend, Val, put me in charge. And I decide for you!" He stepped closer glaring at me intensely.

"Oh, you think you can exert your authority?" my hands flew to his chest and shoved him hard, my voice just below a bellow. "Val doesn't own me nor do you!" I paused, calming my tone. "Sally's body is a message. If I don't go after Jeffery and Dom then they are as good as dead."

The Cajun roared, throwing his hand on my shoulder in a possessive manner. "They are already dead! That's why this wild goose chase is a waste of time."

"That's not true!" I refuted. "If they were already dead don't you think Aidan would've left their bodies instead of Sally's remains?"

"I can't say. It is very hard gauging a maniac." The Cajun bit out through his teeth.

"I know you don't want to hear this, but if there is a chance in hell that the guys are still alive, I have to try. I owe them that much. This is my entire fault!"

"How is this your fault?"

"The Illuminati owns me. I am their slave. I will never belong to myself and as long as I run from those insidious bastards, anyone in a five-mile radius of me is not safe."

A shiver of uncertainty glinted in the Cajun's dark eyes. He stalled capturing my gaze to his. "If you go, then I go with you!"

"This idea isn't any better than me running. I can't have you risk your life too. Right now, you are all I have. I don't want to lose you too."

"All the more reason I should go with you, *yes?*" He retorted with determination that forbade any further argument.

CHAPTER 13

THE POINT OF NO RETURN

*O*ff we rolled in the hummer loaded down with our homemade bombs and even jugs of moonshine. Since we were looking down the barrel of advance alien weaponry, we needed as much muscle as we could muster. If it could kill the regulators, then I wanted to stockpile every cleansing chemical underneath the sink and moonshine to the heavens. It's like a skinny man sparring with a heavy weight boxer on steroids. We had to fight dirty. Personally, I never knew a fight that wasn't.

We'd grabbed up can goods and other foods that didn't require refrigeration. I found in the pantry a large box of beef jerky. We hit the jackpot with that. Dried jerky didn't spoil. We could eat on it forever.

To add to our survival list, we collected every empty container that we could find and filled them with clean water. For now, we were okay. I reckoned that was as good as it gets these days. All we could do was count our blessings and stay alive.

The honeycomb sun had crest the horizon. There was promise of another unusually hot sultry day. The atmosphere was taut, unyielding.

This time I felt a bit more protected in this huge tank. The tinted windows gave us a sense of protection. And the renowned symbol, the knowing eye, on the plates, I felt hopeful that we'd pass for Illuminist, slipping past their dirty noses. Of course, this was all in theory.

The Cajun insisted on driving. I wasn't up for the challenge to argue, so I didn't put up a fight. In fact, I actually felt relieved when he took over the wheel. He knew the town better than I did and he'd had experience, during his tour in Afghanistan, driving heavy-duty tankers similar to the Hummer.

The wheels churned in my ear as my heart joined, pounding my chest when we entered Bourbon Street. A stark silence lingered between us.

My teeth were on edge as I gripped my seat. The Cajun's gaze was as intense as a mountain lion hunting for prey. He kept combing the street for any signs of trouble.

Not much had changed since last night. Similar to the day after the Mardi Gras, the street was cluttered. The only proof of life left was the tons of debris, scurrying in the wind and collecting at the curbside. The air had a pungent odor of garbage, feces and something else that I couldn't put my finger on. It was almost as bad as Sally's decaying body.

Almost.

I wringed my hands, feeling like a cat in ice water scrambling for a dry surface. I glanced at the Cajun and then back to street. I felt responsible for him. I blamed Val. He should've never given Nick the burden of protecting me. Having me for a partner was like sitting on a live grenade. You knew it was going to explode, you just didn't know exactly when. I wished he's gone his way but he was too bullheaded to listen to reason. So here we were about to bite off more than we could chew.

Another frightening thought, knowing how much the Illuminist loved experimenting, creating genetic freaks like me; I feared the regulators were small fries compared to a much larger picture. I recalled how Aidan boasted about super-soldiers. No telling what kind of monsters the Illuminist planned springing on us. I didn't want to think about the peril that awaits. I was already on the ledge ready to jump. Despite my frail mind, I had to face the possibilities and prepare myself for the worst. The Illuminist had the control, and we were the roaches that they intended to exterminate.

We rolled into downtown on Bourbon Street, a line of locals had started to gather on the sidewalk. They must be getting food rations. I spotted stacks of brown boxes against a brick building.

My pulse lurched when I spotted two regulators. One stood at the front of the line, checking each person's wrist. Another regulator was herding the growing crowd, aiming his weapon and shouting at them to form a line.

An elderly woman suddenly emerged from the line. She appeared lost. I watched as she clenched her cane for support, creeping across the street. Just like the others, the woman had the same dazed expression.

Suddenly the regulator cut his attention to the woman. He shouted at her, but she continued edging her way to the other side of the street.

Angry fowl words spilled from the creature's mouth as he abruptly aimed and fired his weapon, shooting the elderly woman in cold blood.

Her body went limp, crashing to the pavement headfirst. Like a watermelon bursting, a loud thud pierced the air. Crimson blood pooled around the crumpled body.

My hands flew to my mouth unconsciously, eyes wide.

In the next breath, drones exact duplicates of the ones that attacked me, swooped in and hovered over the woman's limp body as if they were collecting data. Seconds later, they zipped across the sky vanishing behind a strange gray cloud.

I stuttered in horror, "H-h-he just shot her!" out of my mind, I half shrieked rushing for my door. The Cajun swiftly grabbed my upper arm, his fingers biting into my skin.

I snapped my eyes back at him and hissed,

"I have to stop that creature from killing anyone else!" Tears filled my eyes.

"*Non*! You can't help her or any of those people." His voice lulled me back to my senses.

I settled back into my seat, giving him a curt nod. Once he dropped his hand, I swiped the tears from my eyes. He was right. I couldn't save her. I couldn't save any of them.

The Cajun and I shared in an icy silence as we eased down the street.

Chills spiked down my spine as I watched from my side window. Not taking another glance at the old woman's body, the regulator stalked back to the line. He displayed no concern, not even giving it a thought to his injustice, murdering a defenseless old woman. He left her there for the birds to pick. I wanted to vomit.

Chills slithered across my neck as my eyes spread over the crowd. They all stood with blank faces, staring at the front of the line. It was as if the crowd was void of any natural emotions. Not one person acknowledged that an execution had just befallen.

Shock, fright and anger pummeled me. The regulator's deliberate cruelty didn't make sense. The woman wasn't resisting. She was merely confused.

In fact, everything about this picture left me disconcerted. They all wore the same far-off-distant, blank face as if they'd had a lobotomy or underwent one too many shock treatments. It became evident to me just how sickly these people were. As I noted the black circles that embellished their dull eyes and their pale skin that sagged off their bones, I knew that they were only a breath away from death. The worse part was the children. Large eyes sunk back into their small skulls, staring absent-mindedly, cheeks hollowed, no more than an empty shell of the children they once were, jumping and running, little voices full of laughter.

At that moment, I'd never felt more useless, watching innocent men, women and children getting treated worse than animals. I was furious with myself and enraged at these monsters that called their barbarian justice.

My heart was breaking knowing I couldn't do anything to help. Could anyone save the suffering? No one had the power to fight against this atrocity. Not one person! Not even a genetic angel! I sighed with overwhelming grief.

While we edged closer to Val's place, I kept my eyes on the increasing number of locals piling in line and stretching several blocks down at this point. Geez! I got the impression that the whole city had depended on the food rations. I didn't like this one bit.

I noticed that several folks wore the same tattoo on their wrist. When we rolled by a man making his way to the line, I got a good look at his mark.

When I realized what was happening, I gasped with a start. "Oh, my God!" I mumbled. The Cajun's friend, Toe, was right. The Illuminist was inking everyone with the mark of the beast. Numbers 666, mankind's imprisonment. Of course, the Order took away all food sources forcing the people to become dependent on them for stables and clean water. But only those who receive the ink would be given the free rations. My stomach roiled just thinking about the lengths these devils would go. The Order is sweeping the world by medicating humanity through their most basic needs.

I rushed my words at Nick, "I think I know what they are doing."

"What are you talking about?"

"The Illuminati are using the ink to control the people!" My words heightened.

"Shush! Keep it down," he growled in a low voice.

"Those numbers on the wrist are implants, tags. They use the implants to hinge these people into a state of hypnosis!"

The Cajun stiffened. "*Merde*! I wouldn't put anything passed those fucking bastards."

"They're killing the people by poisoning them with the food." I crossed my arms, eyeballing the regulator that had shot down the old woman. I wanted to murder him with my bare hands.

The Cajun rubbed absently at his right arm, "How can you be certain? It's possible that they are starving, yes?"

I jerked my gaze to his, "Nick, think about it!" I did a mock thump to his forehead. "What better way to wipe out a civilization than poisoning their water supply and food?"

The Cajun shifted in his seat and blew out a disparaging breath. "Even if you are right, it makes no matter? We can't help them. They're already dead. Look at them." The Cajun nodded to crowd. "They are not much more than ghost in human flesh. That's all the more reason why we need to get what we came for and get the fuck out of here."

I think at that point, we both sensed an unfathomable end, terrified for what was to come and this was only the beginning. The beginning of the apocalypse.

~

We parked at the curb in front of Val's place. Unlike the Jeep, the Hummer was too burly to fit under the stairwell. I reckoned it was a risk we had to take. Thank goodness, the Hummer looked like one of the vehicles the Order used.

I reached for my door when the Cajun halted me with an iron grip on the wrist. My gaze caught his and I paused, confused.

Dipping his head closer to my face, he spoke in a low voice. "You need to pull yourself together. We can't show any emotion or our cover will be blown. Moi je comprends-vous? (Do you understand me?)" his jaw clenched, his eyes slightly narrowed.

"I've got this!" I shrugged, withdrawing my hand.

One corner of his mouth tugged into a smile. "C'est ma fille! (That's my girl!)"

With my knives strapped underneath my clothes, hidden, I followed the Cajun's lead, sliding out of the car and casually made my way to his side. Our eyes stayed alert to any possible threat.

When I stepped into a downwind, I instantly picked up a pungent odor. Disgust hit me as I spied the side of Val's bar where splattered piss decorated the building, along with clumps of feces soiling the sidewalk.

I cupped my mouth, gagging involuntarily. The Cajun grabbed my elbow roughly, as he leaned into me. He smiled against my ear, whispering in a low harsh voice. "Pull your shit together before you get us both killed."

I dropped my hands to my side and smiled back at the Cajun as if we were lovers. I hated that he was right. Any natural reaction to the creatures' insidious behavior would bring unwanted attention. I needed to be more careful. We couldn't afford any more slipups.

I swiped a quick glanced back down the street where we'd drove past the two regulators and the increasing crowd of locals. The two guards were plenty busy passing out food-boxes to the locals to pay any mind to our presence. A little spurt of hope bristled my neck. We might pull this off after all.

We stopped at the door to Val's gym. My pulse erratically pounded in my ears. It was the only part of me that wasn't numb. I shared a terse glance with the Cajun.

He brusquely nudged my shoulder. "Use your magic. Open the door."

I nodded, stepping up and wringing my fingers around the door handle. I first turned the handle, hoping that Val might've left the gym unlocked. To my disappointment, the handle didn't budge.

Realizing we had only minutes left, I began to invoke my essence. I closed my eyes focusing on the lock. A sudden spark of warmth shot through me, reaching my tingling palm. In the next half breath, the handle gave under my grasp.

I smiled up at the Cajun as he pressed the small of my back for me to move inside.

Blood rushed to my head as I eased the door open. With caution, I stepped inside. Alert to any surprises, my knives hovered above my head cocked, ready to spring into action. The Cajun stayed on my heels, eyes watchful to any signs of trouble, fingering his pistol, sheath to his hip as he shut the door behind us.

Plunged into darkness, we paused just passed the entrance. The Cajun pulled out of his pockedt a small flashlight and flipped it on, shining the small stream of light out into the vast gym. The light only reached a small distance, but it was better than groping through the dark.

The Cajun leaned in my ear. "Do you even know what you're looking for?" He grated.

"I'll know when I see it," I snapped in a hushed voice.

"You better hurry! Time is running out," he whispered over my shoulder.

Frustrated, I snatched the flashlight from the Cajun's hand and ventured my way to the very back where Val had his collection of sorted weapons cased.

When I stopped, I shined the light on the wall, but Val's collection of swords were gone, only a blank canvas. I didn't know why I was surprised. Val wouldn't have left his valuable collections for the regulators to destroy.

I twirled on my heels facing Nick. "There's nothing here!" my voice broke. Did I risk both our lives coming here?

The Cajun grabbed the flashlight from my hand and swiped the room over and stopped on a glass case sitting off by itself. "What about this?"

My eyes followed the dim light and a burst of excitement struck. "The spear!" I half mumbled, running to its side.

Nick followed shortly behind me.

I stood with my palms on the glass peering through to the spear. "That is so strange for Val to leave this behind."

"It looks old. What's so great about this?"

My eyes hitched to Nick's. "It is ancient. It's called the Sword of Destiny." I swallowed. "It's the same spear that pierced Jesus Christ."

"What a sick fuck to keep such an evil thing." Nick blew out a harsh sigh.

"No! Val was keeping it safe and out of the hands of the Illuminati. Do you know if this spear ever got into their hands, they would be unstoppable?"

"All the more reason we should destroy it."

"We can't. It's cursed with dark enchantments."

"Merci! Ne jamais s'arrêter cette folie? (Mercy! Will this madness ever stop?)" The Cajun flurried a string of French curses.

I brushed the stream of light over the spear and stopped.

"Nick!" I could hardly breathe. "I found our next clue."

The Cajun stepped up and followed the light. "Another note!"

"Yes!" hope charged through me. "Give me your gun." I held out my palm, but keeping my eyes on the note that laid at the base of the spear.

"*Non!* No way are you going to fire a gun and alert those shit-dropping regulators."

I turned to Nick, facing him. "I don't want to fire the gun. I want to break the glass." I hissed.

The Cajun paused, soaking in my stern gaze. "You don't want to touch that spear."

I huffed. "Just give me the gun." I glared at him as I held out my palm.

The Cajun grumbled to himself. "Move! I'll do it." he pulled out the pistol and gently shoved me to the side.

He struck the glass with the grip of the gun. Glass went shattering, smashing onto the concrete floor into tiny shards. Nick reached in and drew out the note. "You read it." he shoved the note into my hand.

A quiver in my stomach seized my breath as I paused for a brief moment, staring at the note. Dragging in the air born dust, I opened the note and began to read,

Dear Stevie and your comrade, Nick,

I hope you both had a wonderful stay at my

home. I hope it wasn't too disturbing when you found Sally. I'm truly sorry for the mess. I simply no longer needed her services. By now, I am quite certain you must be wondering if your love ones are safe and alive. I assure you they are still breathing. Although, I regret to inform you that your friends are in a place you cannot reach. I am sure you have heard of its existence… the floating castle.

I understand you have rather a difficult time traveling out of your dimension. It will be very interesting to see if you can hurdle this task. Hope to see you soon, for time is of the essence. No punt intended.

Oh, yes. Just to make things more interesting, I decided to throw in another challenge. You are in the throes of an attack. I fear my sweet darling that you and your Arcadian friend have walked into a trap.

Sincerely,
Aidan

The Cajun raked his fingers through his disheveled curls, more curses streamed from his mouth. "Let's get out of here and now!" he half shouted.

"Wait!" I called out. I reached in and snatched up the spear. "We can't leave this behind."

"*Non*! It's cursed. You said yourself."

"I'm not leaving it!" I bit down on my words. I'd take my chances with the spear than risk it ending in the wrong hands.

"Come on! No time to argue with you, gul." He tugged my arm, dragging me along with him.

The Cajun stopped at the entrance and pressed his ear against the door, listening. I stood beside him waiting for him to signal to go.

After what felt like an eternity, he waved his finger for me to proceed.

I eased out the door, combing my glaze over the street. The Cajun was right behind me. I could feel his warm breath on my shoulder.

We paused under the stairwell, checking if the close was clear. Neither one of us spotted possible trouble as we scurried for the Hummer.

The Cajun had the keys in his hands ready. He punched the remote, unlocking the Hummer. Not wasting a beat, I dove in on his side and swiftly climbed over to my seat. I rushed to buckle up as the Cajun slid behind the wheel, slamming the key in the ignition.

In one quick motion, Nick turned the key but the motor stalled. "Damn!" he grated curses. He pumped the gas and turned the key. The motor dragged, slowly churning.

"It sounds like the battery's dead."

"*Merde*! Someone fucked with the motor while we were inside." Nick pounded his fist against the wheel, French curse words spewed.

He threw the door open and started to step out but he halted. The street began to rumble. Not like an earthquake but like an army of heavy feet stomping.

Nick and I shared a wary glance as the sound increased.

Then the reality of our peril reared its ugly head. A rumble stronger than the one before vibrated the Hummer. I grabbed the handle above my head to hang on.

When my eyes lifted, sheer panic iced me to the bone. Approaching fast coming around the corner where we entered Bourbon Street, I saw marching men in gray uniform.

Soldiers!

These men were not your run of the mill troopers. They were massive in size, ten feet or better with weapons that equally matched their size.

Each synchronized step they took, the vibration grew stronger. The Hummer began shaking, bouncing off the curb. I compared it to the Great Chilean Earthquake.

I knew with certainty that Aidan had been sending me on a wild goose chase, and I had myself to blame for this. I had led Nick into this insidious trap.

"Nick! We've got to get this car moving!" my voice carried over the stepping feet.

"What the fuck you think I'm doing!" he bit back.

Think Stevie, think, I said to myself. "Nick let me in the driver's seat!" I urged.

The Cajun glared at me like I'd lost my mind. Maybe he was right.

"Nick! Give me the wheel *now*!" I insisted. Time was running out. The infantry of men were approaching upon us fast. I knew exactly what we were about to confront...*the Nephilim*. Hybrid giants of their ancestors. Aidan had warned me of such and now I wish I'd listened.

"Nick! I can start the car."

After a sour glare, the Cajun snatched me up and slid me over him as we swapped seats.

"I hope you know what you're doing." The Cajun scowled.

I ignored his comment, "Be quiet. I have to concentrate." I placed my hands on the stirring wheel and closed my eyes. I pushed for my essence and slowly it rose. Soon my hands were glowing and I felt the warmth from my hands to the wheel as it continued to weave its magick throughout the metal of the hummer.

"You better hurry! Or else we're going to become those giants' fucking meal." The Cajun growled as he gathered more grenades from the back.

"I know! I know already!" I repeated, as fright surged through me like ice. I pushed my essence even harder as the engine started to kick. Churning and churning and finally the engine turned and the Hummer was purring like new.

"*Merde*! Let's get this baby rolling!"

He didn't have to ask me twice. I put the petal to the metal and peeled out. The Hummer's motor revved as I gunned it down the street heading in the opposite direction.

Nick kept his eyes peeled, if the giants or anything was gaining.

Then suddenly, my heart stopped. I hit the brakes as we went into a tailspin. The hummer hit the curb and nearly flipped over but it managed to land back on its wheels with a hard thud. "Dammit!" I cursed. The Cajun and I gaped at the sight before us. "Those cold heartless bastards did the unthinkable. Innocent men, women and children stood as a barrier blocking our path!"

"I've seen this before. They're banking on your humanity. Those sick fucks will stoop to whatever it takes." Nick sneered.

I glanced back to go the other way but the giants and regulators had other folks barricading the other end of the street too. "I can't run those people over!" I shouted at the Cajun.

"Give me the wheel!" he commanded.

"*No*! I won't let you hurt these people."

"*Non*! We don't have time for debate! Give me the fucking wheel!"

I glared at him.

"Come on! We ain't got time to argue, gul!"

I paused biting my lip hard. "Fine! Take the wheel." I opened the door and started to step out.

The Cajun halted me by clasping his fingers around my arm. "What the fuck are *you* doing?" His face said it all.

I was one crazy bitch tempting fate.

"I'm going to distract them while *you* escape."

"*Non!* I can't let you commit suicide." his jaw twitched.

"It's all we got. Look! I can handle it. Whatever they dish out, I can dish back. That's what I was designed for… *to fight!*" I reasoned.

"You can't fight a whole army, gul!"

My voice calmed, "I don't plan to. I'm giving myself up."

A trail of curses flew from the Cajun as he ran his fingers through his thick hair. "Why would you want to do such a cuckoo thing?"

"It's the only way I can save you and these people. Besides, if I can get inside, I have a chance of finding the guys."

"I don't like this one damn bit!" Nick growled.

"You knew we were going to part ways sooner or later." I glanced back at the encroaching troops. For every second we stalled, the soldiers drew closer. There was no time to argue. I expected any minute now that they'd take us hostage and it'd be too late for the Cajun. They'd kill him and maybe kill me too.

Then I did something that had not crossed my mind or entered my heart. Maybe it was his soulful eyes pleading, or just the craziness of facing death, but I reached over weaving my hands through his thick curls and laid one tongue thrashing kiss right on him. At first, he stiffened, and then soon he returned the kiss with as much passion as I gave him. When we pulled away, we both were short of breath. Our eyes connected as we shared a golden moment of farewell. No words were needed. We both knew this was the end of the line.

With a smothered groan, the Cajun let go of my arm and I stepped out of the Hummer. My hands raised above my head, I sauntered over to the encroaching giants and their comrades, the regulators. I halted in the center of the street.

Behind me, I heard wheels peeling. The smell of rubber burning assaulted my nose. Then I heard glass shattering and the crashing of a building crumbling. I smiled to myself. The Cajun did exactly what he said he'd do. A calm sense came over me knowing he'd gotten away. They didn't want him anyway. The Order wanted me.

Yet I was disappointed that Aidan wasn't leading the pack. What I'd do right now if I could get my hands on him.

I tried not to flinch but I couldn't stop myself as I closed my eyes waiting for my fate.

The next thing I heard was harsh murmurs. Several ironclad hands accosted me roughly, pulling me a part like a medieval rack, ankles and wrists bound, stretching my limbs until they snap.

Then the unfathomable pain stopped after a sudden blow to the back of my head and my world went black.

Dear reader,

We hope you enjoyed reading *Deviant Angel*. Please take a moment to leave a review, even if it's a short one. Your opinion is important to us.

Discover more books by Jo Wilde at

https://www.nextchapter.pub/authors/jo-wilde

Want to know when one of our books is free or discounted? Join the newsletter at

http://eepurl.com/bqqB3H

Best regards,

Jo Wilde and the Next Chapter Team